WILD IRISH DREAMER

BOOK 8 IN THE MYSTIC COVE SERIES

TRICIA O'MALLEY

LOVEWRITE PUBLISHING

"You may say I'm a dreamer,
But I'm not the only one." – John Lennon

CHAPTER 1

ou almost lost him.

      Fi awoke in a sweaty mess of sheets, her heart hammering in her chest, her mind stuck in the boggy ground between waking and sleep. Having shot upright at the voice that raged in her dream, she now plopped back to her pillows, gasping, and attempted to sift through the images that threatened to slip from her mind. It was the cove, she was sure of that, for no dreams ever spoke to her as vividly as the ones that came from the enchanted waters in the cove. The problem was, this wasn't her first time – and likely not her last – having prophetic dreams involving her hometown.

It was her bloodline that had enchanted the waters there, after all.

It was probably just another dumb tourist who refused to listen to the advice of the locals. Fi sighed and rubbed a hand over her face, willing her breathing to calm down. Every year, someone was seriously injured at the cove. Despite the posted warnings, despite the local people educating visitors about the vicious undertow, someone always insisted on trying to venture down the steep trail to the deceptively tranquil beach in the cove. They quickly learned their mistake, they *always* did, but sometimes at a steep price.

The cove was magickal, as was her blood, a gift which Fi often did her best to suppress. It wasn't that she detested what had been passed down to her through her bloodline – it was more that Fi just wanted to do everything on her own. She'd been like that since she came screaming from her mother's womb, ready to take on the world, and nobody could tell her differently. Sometimes the gifts of magick that had been passed down from the great Grace O'Malley herself came in useful for Fi, but for the most part, she tried to ignore them; it was vitally important to her that she conquer the world without any extra help.

The dreams, though – those were another story.

"Who am I losing?" Fi demanded out loud, closing her eyes and willing herself to see. Of course, the one time she *did* want her gifts to work, all she could get was vague snatches of the cove and someone in incredible pain. Worried it could be someone close, Fi checked the time and picked up her phone.

"Aye, and to what do I owe this pleasure? Me own wayward daughter, running about the world with not a moment to call her mum."

Fi grinned at Cait's words through the phone, having just spoken with her two days ago.

"I'm positively a stranger these days, I am. 'Tis a right shame I bring to the family," Fi agreed.

"Your father is convinced you've become a groupie to a band and have gone to drugs now."

"A groupie? That's insulting. I'd start me own band, that's the truth of it," Fi scoffed, offended that her father would think she'd just blindly follow some deadbeat musicians around the world.

"Ah, so it's just the drugs then," Cait said.

"Naturally. But I just sell them. It's how I fund this fancy lifestyle of mine. But I don't use. Never get high on your own supply, as they say," Fi said, stretching her legs out and letting her mum's voice soothe her pounding heart.

"'Tis the smartest way. It's why I've only a nip or two of the whiskey when I'm working," Cait agreed.

"Is… everything okay?" Fi asked, closing her eyes so she could read her mother's voice.

"I believe it to be. Have you had a dream then?"

"Aye, about the cove. Maybe have someone give it a check and make sure another tourist hasn't ended up down there?"

"Shane, your daughter says check the cove. Have a call over there, will ye?"

"Tell her to come home."

"She'll come when she's ready."

"Tell him I'll be home for Grace's hen party soon," Fi promised.

"Oh, right. Have you ideas for it then?"

"I do…"

Fi spent the next half hour chatting comfortably with her mum while the anxiety drifted from her neck and shoulders. All seemed to be well at the cove, so Fi shrugged it off as an odd dream and left it at that. No need to search for more troubles – she already had enough on her plate. Speaking of which, she needed to finish her project for today so she could spend the rest of the day shopping for supplies for Grace's party. But first, coffee.

In the time since she'd been living on the Amalfi Coast, Fi had learned to love strong coffee like her Italian neighbors, though she preferred to linger over it on her small terrace overlooking the water if the weather was nice instead of taking it like a shot at the counter of the coffee shop below. Try as she might, Fi had never mastered the art of waking quickly, and she'd learned to build time into her mornings to ease into the day and wake her brain up. Fi now took this routine to sit by her window where she could read the paper – yes, the actual paper – and savor her morning espresso.

As a translator specializing in Italian, Spanish, and French, Fi thought it necessary to immerse herself where she worked. Hence the Italian paper, which she read every morning, front to back. It helped to loosen her mind and get her thinking in Italian, after which she could sit down to whatever contract she was translating and work with confidence.

Today, though, her brain struggled to focus. Inexplicably, she was drawn back to the memory of a man whose image periodically drifted through her mind. Liam Mulder. She wondered where he was these days.

She hadn't been long out of university when she'd first met him. Fi thought back, closing her eyes and tipping her face up to the sun that struggled to shine through the clouds.

She'd been green, eager for work, and ready to take on

the world. Sean Burke, Margaret's husband and kin to Fi, had hired her to translate a contract for his shipping company up in Dublin. Fi still remembered her first day: Dressed in a smart black suit and wearing sky-high red heels, she'd walked into the meeting and realized just how egregiously overdressed she was. Scattered around the table were a slew of men in denim pants and button-down shirts, sleeves casually rolled to their elbows. Immediately recognizing her dismay, Sean had welcomed her and put her at ease, a warning look in his eyes for the others. Only Liam had smiled widely at her, including her in on the joke she'd made of herself. She'd immediately taken to him.

Through their negotiations – Sean was acquiring two new ships from an Italian shipping company – Fi had found herself laughing and chatting with Liam. There was something about the careless confidence he'd exuded that had pulled Fi in.

When he'd invited her for a drink after work, Fi had eagerly accepted. But when she arrived back at Sean's house, where she'd been staying the night to catch up with him and Margaret, he had called to cancel.

"Work conflicts," Liam had said, apologizing gracefully.

"It's not our time," Fi had replied, then pulled the phone away to look at it in shock. Where had that come from?

"Is that so? Well, you'll have to let me know when it is," Liam had said, and Fi had hung up, her cheeks flushed with embarrassment. What was wrong with her?

"That Liam?" Sean had asked, watching her carefully from across the table.

"Aye, that was. He called off meeting up tonight." Fi shrugged.

"That's a lad. Wouldn't want to mix business and pleasure," Sean had said, and then gruffly changed the subject. That was when Fi had realized Sean had scared Liam off.

Goddess save her from overbearing family. Vowing then and there to follow her dream of being independent and traveling the world, Fi had eagerly accepted the next client project that allowed her to travel. Off she'd gone, and Liam had faded into the past.

Just a memory... or so she'd thought.

CHAPTER 2

𝓘t must have been six or so years before she'd happened upon Liam once again. It was completely by chance, as things often are, and Fi almost hadn't recognized him when he'd pulled up a chair at the little table where she was sitting outside a small restaurant on a back street in Pula, Croatia. Glancing up, she'd composed her face into a coolly distant look, ready to dismiss whoever had dared to interrupt her rare moment of alone time.

"Fi?"

"Ah… yes? Oh my – Liam, right?" Fi had asked, a delighted grin stealing across her face.

"Correct. I thought that might be you, but I had to do a double take. You've cut your hair," Liam said, crossing his arms over his chest.

"And you've grown yours." Fi smiled once more, leaning back into her chair and studying him. He'd grown, she realized, in more ways than one. He was more masculine now, with a scruff of beard and hair a few months past a haircut, and his sea-blue eyes seemed to promise tales of faraway lands.

"Aye, life at sea will do that to a lad, I suppose," Liam said, running a hand through his chestnut hair. With enough time in the sun, Fi imagined, his hair would go to red, but just now it was a deep brown with hints of amber and gold woven through.

"Have you been on the water then? Less time in business meetings, more at sea?"

Liam paused when the waiter stopped at their table, and raised an eyebrow at her as if to ask whether it was all right for him to order. He waited until she gave a small nod, and then ordered enough food to feed ten men, along with two types of wine.

"Will there be more joining us?"

"I've been at sea for the last two weeks, my lady, and the food on board is not quite up to this level. I plan to indulge myself. And since you're here, I'm assuming you're hungry as well, so I took the liberty of ordering for us both."

"How do you know I didn't already order?"

"No bother then, I'll eat your share as well." Liam had smiled and Fi found herself charmed by him.

"I haven't yet ordered my food, so I'll take you up on your non-invitation to dinner."

"See? And since I didn't invite you to dinner, then Sean can't run me off again," Liam said, nodding his thanks to the waiter who deposited red wine and two glasses on their table, along with a basket of bread. "May I?"

"You may," Fi said, tilting her head to look at Liam's

face. "So it *was* Sean who made you change your mind that time you asked me for a drink."

"That it was. I can't be blaming him, either. I think every man in the room would have given it a go if Sean hadn't laid down the law."

"Given it a go?" Fi raised a delicate eyebrow at the phrase.

"Sure. Taken a chance on asking you out. I was the only one ballsy enough to try. I like taking risks though." Liam held up his glass and Fi automatically did the same with hers, clinking it gently against his.

"Slainté."

"And yet, you still canceled on me," Fi said, sipping the wine and letting the flavors roll over her tongue. Her cheeks felt flushed – not from the wine, but rather the frank appreciation in Liam's gaze upon her.

"Aye, 'tis true, I did. I didn't realize the family connection until later. As Sean was a colleague, I had to respect his wishes. It's not a bad thing, either. I've learned over the years to never mix business and pleasure. It inevitably muddies the waters, and it's never worth it."

"Is that so? I'm inclined to agree, but I'm a curious sort, Liam," Fi said, leaning over to pick a piece of rosemary bread from the basket. "Care to tell me how you learned that lesson?"

"I'd be lying if I said I learned it right away. It took me a round or two to hammer it home – the most recent one being the worst of them. I think that's me done with working with my romantic partners, and that's the truth of it."

Fi paused, reading real pain in his eyes. Keeping her

mental shields up, as she didn't want to pry into his thoughts, she waited. Her mother had taught her at a young age that their gift of reading others' thoughts was not something to be used in a harmful or disrespectful manner. She'd borne the brunt of a few disgruntled outbursts when she'd spoken other people's thoughts in the shops as a child.

"Silence? I see you've learned a few things at the negotiating table." Liam sighed and leaned back in his chair, running one hand over the scruff on his chin. "Her name was Vera and she was working the financials on a recent shipping contract I was project-managing. Despite myself, I was drawn to her and crossed the boundary. We dated for over a year – quite seriously, I thought."

"Where is Vera from?"

"She's Russian."

"Were you working in Russia?"

"No, here in Croatia. We've been contracted here for almost a year. I... I thought there was more to the relationship than there was."

Despite her best efforts, Fi got a mental flash of a ring box and Liam standing outside a doorway.

"I'm sorry to hear that. Do you want to tell me what happened?" Fi asked. She nodded when he held up the bottle to top off her wine glass.

"I was taken for a ride," Liam said, and then paused, draining his glass and filling it once more. He grimaced and looked out across the street, pain slicing across his face before he shook it off. "It hurts to admit that more than anything, I think. I'm usually such a good judge of character."

"Love can blind us," Fi said, reaching out to pat his arm.

"Aye. That it did."

"She cheated?"

"No. Well, at least not that I know of." Liam shrugged. "But I overheard her having a conversation on the phone. They were very clearly discussing how much money I make."

"Okay," Fi said, sipping her drink and tapping a finger on her glass as she thought about it, "but that's not entirely unusual. Even though there's been a shift in the mentality that the man has to take care of the woman, and I am *all* for women supporting themselves, I can see where her friends might want to be sure she was provided for."

"It wasn't quite like that. They were discussing bank accounts. And numbers. And what accounts to drain and wire money to."

"Oh," Fi said, stricken. Reaching across the table, she squeezed his hand, "Oh, that's a tough one. I'm sorry. Did they get anything from you?"

"No, I backed away from the door quietly and changed all my info before breaking up with her."

"Smart man. I'm sorry, that I am, Liam. Should we find her and do something decidedly nasty to her?"

Liam chuckled. "You've a bloodlust in you, Fi."

"That I do. I think it's the warrior in me. It's in the blood."

"I like that about you," Liam said.

"Thank you. Just remember it, should you ever get on my bad side," Fi promised.

"I'd like to get… and stay… on your good side." Liam

measured a look heavy with meaning across the table at her and Fi almost rolled her eyes. Of *course* he would try and push his feelings away by pretending to flirt with her.

"Well, you know what they say is the best way to get over a broken heart…"

Liam smiled, a slow languid smile that had heat pulsing low in her stomach.

"What's that, Fi?"

"A pub crawl with your mates. And seeing as I'm your only mate here at the moment, it's on me to handle the job. Let's get you a solid base of food, and then I'm taking you to play pool." Fi let out a delighted laugh when Liam's mouth dropped open.

"Pool."

"Oh yes, pool. Or darts. But first, we need to find a proper pub, and some whiskey. Go on then, let's get some food in you," Fi said, gesturing to the steaming plates the waiter had just delivered to their table. "See if you can keep up."

"Why do I feel like you're about to drink me under the table?"

"Saddle up, boyo."

CHAPTER 3

"The table's not in the best shape," Fi groused. They were in the tiniest corner pub she'd ever seen and she was inspecting the pool table, with its cracked and worn felt. In the corner sat one tired barman, chain-smoking and largely ignoring the tourists who peered in the door and then quickly moved on. Liam, fueled by about half a bottle of whiskey that Fi had all but poured down his throat at the last pub they'd been to, grabbed the cue from her hand.

"Looking for excuses already? Sounds liked you're scared," he said as he bent to rack the balls. The barman watched, a vague spark of interest flaring in his dull eyes.

"You don't scare me, Liam. I was just commenting on the condition of the pool table."

"Spoken like someone who doesn't trust her pool game. I'll have you know that I am quite a good shot," Liam teased, wobbling a little, and narrowing his eyes at her.

"Christ, this'll be like taking candy from a baby. You're three sheets to the wind already."

"Then you shouldn't be having a problem with playing me."

Fi rolled her eyes as the barman lazily flicked the switch on an old sound system. A low pulse of music filled the pub, and her skin tingled when Liam brushed past her.

"I just don't think it's a fair fight," Fi warned.

"Noted," Liam said, lazily chalking the cue. "You to break or me?"

"Have at it, handsome," Fi smiled and choked down a laugh as he teetered on one foot, righted himself, and then managed to break the balls apart in a messy pattern on the table. What he lacked in finesse he surely made up for in enthusiasm, Fi decided as she studied the table.

"You didn't get anything in," she pointed out.

"Sure and you've an eye for details, don't you, sweet Fi?" Liam raised an eyebrow at her.

"I'll go stripes. Corner pocket," Fi said, and set to working the table. Liam crowed as her first ball sank into the pocket. By the fifth, he'd gone silent.

"Seems like you may have played this a few times, Fi."

"Here and there."

"I'd say more than here and there."

"Did I tell you I used to be in a league? I earned a lot of pocket money from those games." Fi walked the table and studied her angles for her last shot. She kicked her foot up so Liam looked dumbly down at her soft leather boots. "Paid for extra purchases like these gorgeous leather boots."

"Sure, those are some smart boots, Fi." Liam winced as

she bent over the table once more. "Aren't you going to let me play at all?"

"You had your chance when I let you break." With that, Fi shot the eight ball into the corner pocket – much to the delight of the barman, who clapped his hands and held up a bottle with a shot glass. "Looks like the winner gets a shot."

"Damn it. I've been hustled by a wee wisp of a lass," Liam grumbled, but then a wide smile broke across his handsome face and Fi caught her breath. Shaking her head, she hooked her arm through his. "Come on then. Shot's on me."

They'd stumbled their way through the windy streets that night, arms wrapped around each other, laughing so hard they cried. When they'd finally reached the door of the small flat Fi was renting, Liam had leaned against it, smiling down at her.

"There. Safely delivered home. I've done my duty," Liam said.

The moment held and Fi looked up at him, the buzz of alcohol and something else holding her there, her gaze on his lips.

"Have you then? Is there anything else you'd like to do?"

"Aye, Fi, you're testing me limits here," Liam said, running a hand through his hair.

"I wonder just how far I can push them." Fi leaned in and nipped at his lip, brushing hers lightly over his, before turning to unlock her door and push it open. "Will you be joining me then?"

Liam paused in the doorway, his head swinging between the street outside and the staircase up to her flat.

"I suppose it would be ungentlemanly of me not to see you all the way to your door," Liam said, following her in.

Fi bit back a smile as they climbed the stairs in silence, the heat and nearness of him burning through her. Once at her door, she quickly unlocked it, then pushed it open and stepped inside, leaving him to decide. When she heard the door click behind her, she turned and smiled.

"Is this a bad idea?" Liam asked, looking huge in the tiny living room of her apartment.

"Likely," Fi said, unzipping her coat and tossing it to the chair.

"I should go."

"Probably." She crossed to him and ran a hand up his chest.

"I like you, Fi."

"I like you too, Liam." Reaching up, she stood on her tiptoes to brush a kiss over his lips once more. Testing him.

"I don't want you to stop liking me."

"Then don't do something that would make me stop liking you." She reached for his hand, tugging him to her miniscule bedroom. A single bed lay tucked under a small window, and Fi flicked on the pretty beaded lamp on the dresser, making light dance across the ceiling like stars.

"Then I promise you'll like this," Liam said, his voice husky as he picked her up. Her breath rushed from her lungs in one excited gasp as he laid her on the bed. His mouth trailed down her neck, nuzzling into her collarbone, as he began to explore. Fi gasped, arching her neck backward, as his hands found her shirt and unbuttoned it. He pulled her wrists over her head, leaving them tangled in their sleeves. Prisoned there, unable to move or touch him, Fi arched once again as his mouth found her breast, naked beneath her shirt, and began a languid exploration.

Heat speared through her as he took his time at her breasts – an area many men bypassed, as she wasn't particularly blessed in that department – and shivered as his teeth scraped a sensitive nipple. The man had a mouth dreams were made of, she decided. Wanting to touch him, she pushed against the hand that held her pinned. Instead, he moved further down her body, flicking the button of her pants open with one hand and tugging them down her hips.

"Liam, I…" Fi began.

He looked up from her waist, his gaze searing hers with its intensity, his breath ragged.

"Let me give you pleasure," Liam whispered.

"But I want to… you…" Fi groaned as he slipped a hand inside her panties and found her, already aching for him.

"Shhh, my spitfire… let me taste you," Liam said, and then Fi could think no more as he found her sweetest spot with his mouth. He sampled her like a fine wine, taking his time with her and bringing her sharply and deliciously to the edge before she careened off, arching against him and gasping out his name.

When he pulled back, Fi smiled at him.

"That was… you do that well," Fi said.

"Giving brings me pleasure. Women are meant to be cherished," Liam said.

Fi reached up to him, her hands at his belt.

"No, not like this," Liam said, and Fi looked at him in confusion. His eyes drooped and in an instant she could read the drink and the pain and the confusion flashing through his mind. "You're... you're special, Fi. Not like this."

"But..." Fi looked down at her naked body and up to him.

"I... can I just hold you? Just like this? I want you to always remember pleasure from this night." Liam looked dead on his feet, and if she'd ever seen a man about to hit the deck, it was now. "I don't want to be alone."

Sighing, Fi stood and kicked her clothes to a corner. Pulling a t-shirt from the drawer, she dropped it over her head.

"Off with your boots then."

Liam gratefully undressed, and as much as Fi wanted to lick her way down his muscular body, she took pity on the exhausted and emotionally drained man. He climbed into bed and pulled her to him so she fit snugly against his chest, and drifted to sleep in a matter of seconds.

In the morning, he was gone.

CHAPTER 4

*H*e'd left a note. Not that it had mattered, as Fi didn't intend to call him. She'd lain awake much of the night fighting the sense of absolute rightness that had crept over her while nestled in his arms. It was as if her heart was telling her she'd found her home – yet Fi's mind urged her to run. Settling down, whether with one man, one town, or one job, was not something that was currently on her agenda.

For a brief moment that morning, she'd allowed herself to feel sad that he was gone. But it was for the best, as she hadn't wanted to form any unnecessary attachments.

I'd like to see you again. I'm sorry for leaving so early, but I have a meeting. I didn't want to wake you. Call me.

She'd crumpled the note up and tossed it in the bin so she wouldn't be tempted to call him. Two weeks later she'd left Croatia, having accepted a new position at a university in France that was translating some Celtic mythology books.

And so her life had continued. There'd been many men

after Liam, though Fi was selective about whom she took to her bed. More than one man had lingered, providing her with companionship and meeting her needs until she tired of them or accepted a new job in another location. It wasn't that she was careless with men, for she enjoyed their company – it was that Fi never let herself take the long slow slide into love. She'd done that – once. And had learned her lesson.

His name had been Brian. They'd met their first year at university. Blinded by the big-city lights of Dublin and Brian's sharp American accent, Fi had fallen in love – and into his bed – with a speed that had astonished her.

Gracie had come down to visit for a weekend and had left worried, with a warning on her lips for Fi to protect herself. But blinded by Brian's smooth words and edgy taste in music, Fi hadn't listened.

She still remembered the day she'd told him about her gift, opening herself to show him the shadows of her soul – things she never shared with anyone. At first, he'd laughed it off. Then he'd been entranced, peppering her with questions for hours. She'd performed for him, hadn't she? All these years later, the memory still rankled. He'd tested her over and over on her ability to read minds and she'd gone right along, thinking it was because he was fascinated with her.

It was only when she met him at his mate's party the next night that she'd realized how wrong she'd been. Walking in, Fi knew immediately something was off. Somebody flipped the switch on the music, and like a bad teen movie, all eyes had landed on her.

"That's the psychic!"

"She's a witch."

"Maybe she'll help me cheat on my exam…"

"Does she know what I'd like to do in bed with her?"

"Think she can read me the lotto numbers?"

The whispers hit her like shards of glass in a hurricane, cutting her from every direction, as her eyes sought Brian. Finally, they landed on him, tucked on a sofa next to a curvy blonde, a smirk on his face.

Fi had walked right over to him, hands on her hips, and stared down at him until he had no choice but to meet her eyes.

"What have you done?" Fi demanded, her heart hammering in her chest as the room fell silent once again. Not that it mattered – she could hear people's thoughts pinging around her head like a manic pinball machine.

"What's the big deal? I thought it was cool," Brian said, shrugging a shoulder and looking away.

"This isn't how you treat people you love," Fi said, blinking back tears, her voice low with fury. "You don't do something like this. It's not right."

"Ah, what's the big deal, Fi?" Brian scoffed, glancing back up at her. In that moment, Fi read in his eyes what she should have allowed herself to read from his thoughts all along. The only person Brian loved was Brian.

"You should be ashamed of yourself," Fi whispered, and then turned to the room. "This man said he loved me. Is this how a man in love should treat someone?"

"How could I love you after you told me about… that?" Brian waved a hand at her head.

"Yeah. Couldn't you just read his mind and see how he felt?" His mate, Luke, set the room laughing. Fi drew a shaky breath, willing the panic back. A tear escaped, dripping down her cheek as she stared Brian down.

"Aww, the freak is crying."

Brian laughed at that, high-fiving his mate, and Fi's sadness turned to rage. It took everything in her power not to lay Brian's secrets bare to the room, but she couldn't resist sharing just one.

"Just like Brian cries after sex."

The room exploded in laughter. Fi caught Brian's horrified look before she turned on her heel, running from the house and their laughter with her heart shattered in her chest.

She'd vowed then and there to keep men at a distance. Being vulnerable just wasn't worth the risk.

The rule had served her well – right up until she'd met Liam. The night she'd lain in his arms, feeling the rightness of him, was still embedded deep in her brain.

Why was Liam on her mind today? Fi wondered as she picked up her paper and her cup and wandered to the kitchen sink. Of all the men she'd been involved with through the years, her time with him had been the shortest. And yet he seemed to have left a lasting impression on her.

"Enough," Fi said out loud, rinsing her cup and placing it in the drying rack. In the bathroom, she squeezed into the shower, lingering under the miniscule shower head and letting the warm water clear the rest of the cobwebs from her mind. Getting out, Fi studied her face in the mirror. Shadows ringed her large eyes, making her look like she'd had a wild night out instead of a listless night of sleep, and her tangle of hair was already beginning to dry.

A moody face, her mother always said. Her father had called her an indignant pixie.

Either way, Fi's emotions always rang out across her face, and today she looked wounded. Sighing, she applied some concealer under her eyes, smudged a smoky liner along her lids, and patted a rosy hue on her lips with her fingers. Considering herself ready for the day, Fi pulled on a trim grey jumper and slim black pants, and slid her feet into the soft leather boots the Italians were such geniuses at creating. Tossing a checkered scarf around her neck, she hitched her leather tote over her shoulder and left her flat, clattering down the six flights of stairs to the busy street below. The stairs had put her off at first, but now, after routinely indulging in the delicious food Italy had to offer, Fi was grateful for the exercise she was forced to endure when returning to her home each day after work.

"*Ciao, bella*," called Fernando, the man who ran the coffee shop just below her flat, as she breezed by. "You never come see me anymore."

"I like to keep my men guessing." Fi blew him a kiss as he laughed after her. Smiling, she swung past the tables lining the sidewalk and sauntered down the cobblestone street, endlessly charmed by the juxtaposition of old and new on the winding streets of this town. Today she just had to help finalize the last contract in a negotiation for a large tour company she was working with and then she was rewarding herself with a holiday. Which meant Fi could take the afternoon to shop and plan for Grace's upcoming hen party.

She was happy for her friend, Fi mused as she turned and pushed open a door to a small building at the end of the street. In fact, she could pat herself on the back for bringing Dylan and Grace back together. If not for Fi, her stubborn cousin would have refused to see Dylan forever and ever, and they'd have missed out on something amazing.

They were good together. It was something that Fi craved – no, demanded; since she had yet to find it, she hadn't made the plunge into love. Pushing such thoughts away as she walked into the reception area, Fi beamed at the trim woman who greeted her, and followed her through to the boardroom, which was done up in deep mahogany and emerald green tones. Fi appreciated the Italians' flair for design; even in corporate workspaces, color was used to add panache. She moved to the stack of documents that waited for her at the end of the table and barely looked up for the rest of the morning, engrossing herself single-mindedly in the task at hand.

It was a trait that had both pleased and frustrated her mother – as a child, Fi had often become so focused on whatever task she was involved in that she missed hearing her mother call her. Her father always said that someone could set the room on fire around Fi and she wouldn't notice until the book she was reading went up in flames. It was like that with her work as well, but now the trait was well-applauded as she always finished her translations on time, and usually earlier than the agreed-upon deadline.

Today was another such day. After she'd finished typing up her report on the slim laptop she'd brought with her in her tote, Fi let out a breath and leaned back in the chair, rolling her neck to ease the tension from her shoulders. Now for the fun stuff – she could plan Gracie's hen party and pack for going home to see her family, who would undoubtedly welcome her like she was the long-lost child who'd forgotten about them.

It had only been six months since she'd last been home, but a lot had changed in that time. Grace had found love, something which still surprised Fi. Not because she didn't think Grace was worthy of love; oh no – she deserved the best man in the world. But Fi had been convinced that hunkering down at her little cottage by the cove was a guaranteed ticket to spinsterhood for Grace. Nevertheless, love had coming knocking – well, bulldozing, if she were to be precise. Still, Dylan and Grace had found their way into love and now Fi wondered if there was something to be said after all for settling in one spot.

"I really must be tired," she said out loud. She stood, packing her things and neatly stacking the folders of contracts. It wasn't like her to crave normalcy – well, that which she termed normalcy: husband, house, a couple of kids.

Saying goodbye to the woman at reception, Fi wandered into the street and checked her phone for directions to the little secondhand shop she'd looked up earlier. It had promised vintage bridal dresses, and that was the theme Fi had decided on for Grace's hen party. Turning the corner, she ignored the calls of various men as she walked past. She'd gotten used to the forward ways of Italian men, and when she was in the right mood she even indulged it, but today it only annoyed her.

The dark red arched door of the vintage shop beckoned her and Fi gratefully dipped inside, ready to enjoy some retail therapy.

"*Ciao, benvenuta.*" An older woman nodded in greeting, her dark hair threaded with grey. She wore a deep green dress and a gold necklace in the design of a snake.

"I'm here to look at your vintage bridal gowns," Fi said, and the woman nodded her head once more, toward a door that led to a room in the back. Appreciating the unfussy nature of the woman, who didn't seem interested in chattering, Fi breezed through the shop to the back room. Two long racks lined each wall, bursting with dresses.

"Oh, wow," Fi crowed, and pulled out a notebook where she'd recorded everyone's sizes. In less than an hour she'd amassed a pile of tulle and sequin that had even the clerk curious.

"Can't decide which one is for you?" the clerk asked, glancing at where Fi had piled the dresses on a chair.

"Nope, those are for my friends. I'll take all of them. I just have to pick mine out," Fi said, strolling up and down the racks. Her eyes finally landed on a dress that looked like it was straight from a dominatrix store, not meant for a vintage bridal shop.

"I think this will do. But I'd like to try it on first."

"That's certainly a choice," the clerk said.

Fi bit back a smile. She didn't have the heart to admit that she was picking the ugliest dresses she could find in order to have a spoof-wedding hen party.

"I'll just be right out," Fi said and carried the dress into the fitting room. Pulling the mustard-yellow curtain closed behind her, she undressed quickly and slipped the dress over her head.

"May I see?"

"Sure," Fi said, not seeing a mirror in the room. She stepped out to where the clerk stood by a long mirror on the wall next to the fitting room curtain.

"It works for you," the clerk said.

Fi almost giggled when she realized the woman was absolutely serious. There was no way she'd ever be caught in... whatever this shiny material was. Then she turned, and her mouth dropped open when she saw herself in the mirror.

It should have been ridiculous. The latex dress, dripping in sequins with a pouf of ruffles at the hem, hugged her body like a second skin. For once in her life, she looked like she had actual curves instead of the boyish figure she always complained to Grace about. Her eyes looked huge in her face, and oddly alluring.

"I... I honestly was not expecting this to look this good," Fi admitted, running a finger over the bodice. "It's really not my style."

"Are these for a hen party?"

"They are. I thought it would be fun if we all dressed up a little ridiculous in dresses that maybe we wouldn't choose for ourselves." There, she was being honest without insulting the woman's entire stock.

"This dress does not look ridiculous on you. However, I bet I can make it so. Give me a moment." Turning, the woman bustled away, and Fi appreciated the fact that she was more interested in making a sale than in what the gowns were being used for. In a moment, the woman returned, her arms piled full with mounds of tulle and lace in a variety of colors.

"A veil," Fi said, and laughed when the woman

plucked the gaudiest one from the top and placed it on her head. They both stared at the mirror, and nodded together.

"Now it is ridiculous. But, I will say: When you marry, look for a dress in this cut. The shape" – the clerk kissed her fingers – "it is meant for you."

"That's a long way out yet," Fi promised her, though she caught herself staring in the mirror, admiring her body in the dress.

"One never knows. Like a lightning strike, love can scorch your heart in an instant."

CHAPTER 5

*G*allagher's Pub wasn't open yet, but those who knew Cait well enough knew that the door was always unlocked in the mornings. Fi paused outside, admiring the new paint job on the shutters and trim that lined the pub's tall narrow windows. Where the pub had once been green and red, now Cait had chosen a cheerful blue with a brilliant gold trim. Fi approved.

"I see the pub's gotten herself a fancy new dress," Fi called as she pushed the door open. Cait's head popped up from behind the bar and for a moment, Fi's heart squeezed. She'd seen her mum behind the long expanse of burnished wood more times than she could ever count. Gallagher's Pub *was* Cait, and in all her travels Fi had never found another pub that hit all the right notes like this one did. Perhaps she wasn't objective, as it was her family's pub, but that was neither here nor there as far as Fi was concerned.

"You're early!" Cait exclaimed, ducking under the passthrough and racing across the room to throw her arms around Fi. They matched each other in height and build, and rocked back and forth in an enthusiastic hug like two maddened pixies.

"I am at that," Fi agreed. "I finished up work a few days early and now my schedule is clear for weeks." She pulled back to study her mum's face. Perhaps a new wrinkle or two around the eyes, but Cait looked as beautiful as ever – if not more so – as she aged. Fi had always admired her mother, not only for her strong backbone and quicksilver mind, but how she'd never let her beauty get in the way of what she wanted. Over the years, Fi had watched many a woman stumble over obsession with their looks, often not realizing they had so much more to offer the world. Perhaps it was the careless way Cait carried herself, as if to say, 'Sure, I'm lovely to look at, but have you read the latest news reports?' Her mum had a wide grasp of knowledge on a dizzying array of subjects, and ran her business with a steel-minded ferocity. Beauty was appreciated, but business acumen was revered. It was a trait that kept Fi on track as a solo entrepreneur.

"We get you for weeks! That's fantastic. Your father has a surprise for you too." Cait turned and whistled sharply over her shoulder, and Fi bit back a grin. It was the same whistle she'd heard for years and it could mean a variety of things, from "It's time to come home for dinner" to "Stop fighting in my pub."

"Oh, is it the long-lost daughter of mine?" Shane said, swinging through the two doors enclosing the kitchen.

"Da!" Fi laughed and embraced him, inhaling the scents of spice and Guinness that meant he was putting a stew together in the back.

"You've lost weight," Shane decided, having pulled back to examine his daughter.

"Impossible. Not in Italy, at least." Fi shrugged off his concerns.

"I've a lovely Guinness stew brewing. You'll have some," Shane ordered.

Fi rolled her eyes. "I can't believe Mum is letting you in the kitchen these days. Don't you have enough to do with all your properties?"

"We've hired a property manager. It's taken a load of work off, I'll admit it," Shane said as they walked toward the bar. The bar was the focal point of Gallagher's Pub, its wood shined to perfection and worn from years of use and love. Behind the bar, bottles lined the wall on glass shelves, and a mirror reflected the restaurant back. Cait had insisted on the mirror so she could keep an eye on her customers at all times. Spreading back from the bar was a long room with cozy nooks and booths, all set up so people could cluster together in private or pull tables together for a night of music. More often than not, people would wander in with their instruments and take up residence in a booth, playing a lively tune for the crowd that inevitably gathered. None of this was ever planned, and there was no schedule posted proclaiming live music. It was just an accepted fact that music was always welcome at Gallagher's, and Cait had left the musicians to sort the details out themselves.

"And put the man right under me feet all day," Cait griped, popping under the passthrough and coming to stand behind the bar. "Tea?"

"Perfect, thanks," Fi said, settling onto a stool and

putting her purse on the bar. There was just something about a pot of Irish tea. She always missed it on her travels.

"You like having me around," Shane argued. "Just look at all the projects I've finished for you."

"I will admit, it has been nice to get a few things fixed here and there. But you're here all the time now."

"And you love it. When I wasn't here, you'd complain about me being too busy."

"Well, I can't have you working yourself into an early grave, can I?"

"Some could say the same of you, working here every night."

Cait waved that away. "'Tis hardly work, is it now? Just pulling a pint or two."

"You're still on your feet long hours."

"Which is good for me health."

"You owe me a holiday. An extended one."

It was always the same with them, Fi thought, smiling as she added a dollop of milk to her tea. They'd bicker back and forth like this for hours if she didn't intervene.

"A holiday sounds lovely, Mum. Have you actually considered it? Who would watch the pub?"

"Patrick would be fine to handle things," Shane pointed out.

"Aye, he would," Cait agreed, "but where would we go?"

"There's so many places to see," Shane said. "What about South America? Or Africa?"

"Could I see elephants?" Cait's face lit up with excitement. "I must say, I've always wanted to see the elephants."

"You could on a safari. I'll look into it," Shane said, pulling out his phone and typing something in.

"There, that's a lovely idea, isn't it? Going to see the elephants," Fi said. "I bet you'll have stories for weeks to tell everyone when you get back."

"Keelin and Flynn just did that world cruise, as you know. Though why they'd go on those monstrous polluting germ-havens, I do not know."

"They are pretty gross, and they're destroying the oceans. You should see them in Italy – tourists just swarm the cities and barely spend any money. If anyone books a cruise thinking they're helping the local economies, they're dead wrong."

"I heard Venice finally got the cruise ships to stop docking at their ports," Shane said.

"Finally. Who would even want to go on those things? You're locked into a schedule, you can barely explore the towns you go to, and you're stuck on a ship with thousands of people." Fi shuddered. "It's my worst nightmare."

"I will say, Keelin and Flynn weren't as charmed by it as they thought they'd be. Even though Flynn's a sailor, well, I guess he thought the experience would be different. He said he felt like he was on a double-decker bus slogging through the ocean."

"Plus, I don't think they were happy to be gone when Gracie was going through that mess with Dylan."

"No, Flynn was about ready to fly back and punch the man," Shane agreed.

"How are they getting on now?" Fi asked.

"Good enough, it seems. Now that all the plans and motives have come to light –"

"And since Dylan made right on gifting Grace with her cottage," Cait interjected.

"– they seem to be getting on maddeningly well," Shane finished.

"That's good, then. I wouldn't want to be on Flynn's bad side," Fi said. "Actually, Keelin's either. They're both a bit scary."

"Formidable would be the word I'd use," Cait chuckled. "Now, tell us your plans for your stay."

"Yes, do we get you for more than a weekend this time?" Shane asked.

"Yes, you do. I've a few weeks here. I have a few proposals I'm considering, but I haven't technically booked another client just yet. I wanted to spend some time here and help Grace with planning her wedding. Do you mind if I stay in one of your apartments out back? I don't want to be under your feet for weeks."

"You're never under our feet." Cait gave Fi a stern look.

"You know what I mean."

"About that," Shane said. He glanced at Cait, who nodded in return. "We have a surprise for you."

"So Mum said. What's this about?"

"It's an early birthday present."

"My birthday isn't for months yet."

"Well, we never know when you'll be home. Either way, shall we go take a look?"

"At what? What have you done?" Fi narrowed her eyes

at Shane, but jumped when Cait smacked her palm hard on the bar.

"No mind-reading, Fi. Let the surprise be a surprise."

"Fine, but you know I hate surprises."

"Which is why we rarely do them for you. Indulge me." Shane slid his arm around her shoulder, squeezing her to him once more.

Fi sighed, leaning into his warmth. "Fine. You may surprise me. Let's see what this is all about, then."

"Grab your coat. We're going back out."

CHAPTER 6

*S*he'd always loved this street.

Keeping her mental shields up so as not to ruin her parents' surprise, Fi wandered the village of Grace's Cove with them, stopping every few minutes to chat with someone they knew. That was the way of things in Grace's Cove, Fi thought, smiling as another neighbor popped her head out of the bakery. There was no bustling about and getting anything done in a timely manner. Everybody knew everybody, and the gossip mill was a demanding mistress. Within the hour, everyone would know she was back in town. It saved her from having to send out text messages, so there was some benefit to the gossip chain.

They'd turned down a cobblestone street that fronted the harbor, where a long row of semi-detached homes and apartments clambered over each other for prime water views. Each place was painted a different color, creating a vibrant and fun atmosphere, and Fi had spent many a day strolling this waterfront walkway and admiring the beauty of her town. That was the thing of it: Although she craved adventure and world travel, her heart of hearts still belonged to Grace's Cove. It would always be home.

"Here we are then," Shane said, stopping in front of a neat two-story building painted a cheerful burnished yellow, its windows and shutters done up in a pretty red trim. Flower boxes lined the windows, though it was still too early in the season for any buds to be peeking out. An arched doorway, painted a shiny red with a doorknocker in the shape of a gargoyle, was tucked to the left of the windows.

"And who lives here?" Fi asked, stepping back to look up at the building. "It's lovely."

"You do," Shane said, barely containing the glee that flashed across his face as he waited for her reaction.

For once in her life, Fi was truly and honestly gobs-macked. It was as if someone had doused her with a bucket of ice water, and she gasped for air.

Cait gripped her hand, worry etching her pretty face. "See, I told ye it would be too much for her." She glared at Shane.

"It's not too much. Just give the lass a chance to catch her breath."

Fi stepped back and looked at the house once more as emotions crashed through her – the most surprising of which was that she *wanted* this house. How could that be? She'd never thought she'd live here full-time. It wasn't time for her to settle, her brain argued, though her heart screamed, "Take it!"

"I… I honestly don't know what to say. You've gone

and left me speechless, you have," Fi said. "You can't possibly mean you're gifting me a house."

"I am. Well, it's more of an apartment building. It's two flats. Want to take a look and I'll tell you what I'm thinking?" Shane asked, pulling a key from his pocket.

"This is prime real estate. On the water. You should keep this for your portfolio," Fi argued.

"Bah, that man has enough properties. He can't even keep them straight." Cait waved her concerns aside.

"That doesn't mean you just give them away," Fi said.

"It does when it's for your daughter." Cait grabbed her hand and tugged her inside the stoop. "Just have a look around before you tell us no."

"This has to be the most extravagant birthday present anyone has ever been given. You can't possibly think I can accept this," Fi protested, refusing to step inside.

Cait turned to Shane. "I told you her pride would stop her."

"You've never let us pay for anything," Shane said, his eyes on Fi. "Not even your rent when you were in uni. You've worked since you were a child, saving and scrimping and never once asking us for anything. We're incredibly proud of you, and it would be an honor if you would let us gift you with this property."

"You don't make it easy for a girl to say no," Fi said, tears springing to her eyes.

"Don't you start," Cait warned.

"I'm not, I'm not." Fi swiped the back of her hand across her eyes. "Well, let's at least have a look at the place then."

"Wonderful. Just have a look around, see what you

think. I'll tell you why I thought of this property for you."
Shane clapped his hands and turned so he faced the entry-
way. The arched door opened to reveal a small entry hall,
with a narrow staircase on the left and a door on the right.
In the hall sat a small table with a pretty ceramic lamp in
shades of blue and cream. "As you can see, the house is
split into two flats. Each is a two-bedroom, two-bathroom
flat with its own kitchen and living space, and there's a
shared backyard garden."

"Two bedrooms and two bathrooms? That's unheard of
around here," Fi said, following her father up the staircase.

"I had extra bathrooms put in years ago. I used to holi-
day-let these and I realized that many couples traveling
together wanted their own bathrooms. They aren't glam-
orous, but they are serviceable."

"You don't need much in a bathroom, really." Cait
shrugged.

"This is the top floor, which I thought you might like
for your own. The layout is different than downstairs.
Have a look," Shane said, unlocking the door and pushing
it open. He waited for Fi to step through.

"Oh," Fi said, holding her hand to her heart.

Sunlight washed the sitting room from the large
windows at the front, making the buttercream-colored
walls warm and inviting. A wide window seat, made for
dreamers, was littered with blue and white cushions, and a
white afghan was folded neatly in the corner. Fi wanted to
curl up there, looking out over the water, and dream the
day away – reading all her favorite books and drinking tea
while watching the world go by below.

In lieu of a sofa, two oversized armchairs in a soft

cream color flanked a circular wooden table. Footstools in cheerful azure patterns were pulled close to the chairs, and a tall floor lamp stood in the corner. Turning, Fi saw that the room extended into an open kitchen area, something unusual for buildings of this age.

"I opened the kitchen as well, thinking whoever cooked here might like to look out to the water," Shane said, walking back to the counter that doubled as a breakfast bar. Past it, a narrow hallway led to what Fi discovered were two neat bedrooms, each with its own window and a double bed, and two small bathrooms. Nothing ostentatious, nothing too fussy, and just perfect for her. He'd chosen well, Fi mused, as she walked silently around the space, somehow knowing that the living space was more important to the apartment than the size of the bedrooms. Anyone who spent time here would live out in this room. Fi wandered back to the window seat.

"Give it a go," Cait said.

Fi pulled herself onto the cushions, tucking her knees under her chin automatically, and stared out the window, her mind racing. Could she accept something of this nature? It was a huge gift.

And it felt like home.

She'd never had this feeling before, Fi realized, this wanting of a space. She'd lived in flats all over the world, including some she'd dearly loved, yet had never felt a desperate need to own the space. But here? This was meant for her.

"I love it," Fi admitted, and both her parents let out cheers. They dropped into the armchairs and beamed at her.

"I told you she would," Shane said.

"Not true. It was my idea," Cait insisted.

"It was most certainly not."

"Was too."

"Children," Fi interrupted, laughing at them, "this doesn't mean I'll be moving home."

"We figured that. Though you know we wish you would. But here's what we were thinking." Shane held up a hand to stop Fi from interrupting. "This will be a great property to have in your portfolio. One thing I've noticed is that you collect many things on your travels."

"Things that get sent back to us and are now cluttering up your room at home," Cait interjected.

"And this could be a place you could put all the things you've acquired. I don't know if you realize that you've been slowly decorating your future home on your travels, but you have."

"Have I really?" The truth slammed into Fi. Here she'd thought she'd been wandering about and not settling, and instead she'd been slowly accumulating a house worth of stuff. "Well, shite."

"So the thought is, you put your stuff here and then you have a place to come home to between clients, and have your own private space."

"The property downstairs is great as a holiday let, or you can rent it long-term if you don't want to fuss with turnovers. It's extra money in your pocket, and a property manager can look after any issues the tenants have."

"I will take it. But!" Fi held up her hand to keep her parents from chattering over her. "The only way I'll take it is if the rent from the flat below goes straight to you."

"No." Shane shook his head. "That's for you."

"I can't wrap my head around a gift like this. This is huge. The only way I'll take it is if you allow me to buy it from you, a month at a time, via rent." Fi met Shane's eyes, a stubborn set to her chin.

"Oh, she's got that look of hers on," Cait whispered.

"You're breaking me heart here, Fi," Shane said, holding his hand to his heart, a wounded expression on his face. "You won't let your own father give you a birthday gift."

"I am letting you. The upstairs apartment is a rent-free space for me to live in and use as a free storage unit. That's a grand gift. The downstairs will be a way to pay you back."

"I don't need your money, darling," Shane pointed out.

"I know you don't. And I know it will likely be years before I pay this house off. But… I just… it's the only way I can accept something of this magnitude."

"She's got your stubbornness." Shane glared at Cait.

"She's got your pride," Cait shot back at him.

"I'm the best of both of you." Fi smiled at him, glancing back out the window at the people hurrying along the street below, trying to escape indoors before the drizzle that now spattered against the window turned into a full-on downpour. Only one person seemed unconcerned by the rain – a man walking casually down the boulevard toward the docks, his broad shoulders tucked inside a canvas coat. Fi tilted her head and studied him, feeling a familiarity about this man and wishing he would look back over his shoulder.

She realized her mum had said something. "I'm sorry, what was that?"

"If we can pry you away from your new favorite space, we thought you'd might like to see downstairs."

"Oh, right, of course." Fi glanced back out the window once more, but the man had disappeared. She shook her head and turned back to smile at her parents, who were all but bouncing on their heels by the door.

"You're the best parents in the world."

"We know," Cait said.

CHAPTER 7

*L*iam whistled his way down to the docks, nodding his hellos to the villagers on his way. He stopped next to a beauty of a boat, lovingly restored and named *The Pirate Queen*.

"Permission to board," he called.

"Aye," Dylan said, popping his head up and waving to him before disappearing below deck again.

Glad he'd worn his boat shoes today – he didn't fancy taking off his shoes and socks in this rain – Liam climbed aboard the ship and swung down the ladder to the galley kitchen below. Reaching up, he swung the small door closed just as the sky unleashed a torrent of rain on the boat.

"Tea?"

"Aye, that'd be grand," Liam said, shrugging off his coat and hanging it on a hook in the corner. The galley kitchen was small but serviceable, and Liam immediately felt at ease as the boat gently rocked under him while the rain pummeled from above.

He'd been landlocked for too long.

"How's everything going then?" Dylan, his boss and best friend, settled across the narrow table from him, a pot of tea and two cups between them. Liam couldn't count the number of times they'd sat just like this – discussing everything from business to their love lives – and he never once took it for granted. It was a blessed life he led, one where he made enough money for his travels, and work he enjoyed. His friendship with Dylan had been the icing on the cake, for not many were allowed into Dylan's inner circle. He'd been burned by people trying to use him for his connections too many times in the past. Over the years the men had settled into an easy friendship built on mutual respect, trust, and affection.

"The project is on track. Mr. Murphy kept his house in fair condition, but with the addition of the pavilion and extended kitchen out back, we're due to open by spring."

"That's great, but I'm asking about personal."

"Oh, me? I'm fine. How about you? Has Gracie run you ragged with wedding planning yet?"

"Ah, deflection, I see." Dylan's eyes studied him over his cup.

"What's that mean?" Liam cocked his head at Dylan in question.

"You didn't answer my question."

"I said I was fine."

"That's not really an answer."

"I'm pretty sure it's an answer."

"It's a fake answer."

"How is being fine a fake answer? I'm always fine. It's

the state in which I operate." Liam ran a hand through his hair.

"You don't seem fine."

"Are we going to paint each other's nails and put face masks on?"

"Maybe. If that's what it takes to get you to tell me what's going on."

"There's nothing going on."

"Should I get Grace's nail varnish then? Pink might be a good color for you."

"You're a pushy one, you know that?"

"I learned it from you, brother," Dylan flashed him a grin.

"I… I don't know what's up. I'm tetchy of late. Like an itch between my shoulder blades I can't quite scratch. There's no one particular thing or another bothering me. I enjoy the project we're working on. It's fun to work on a passion project and do something a little different for once. I love that you're building something as meaningful as a community center, and the town is as excited about it as we are to be building it. It's probably the most feel-good project I've ever managed."

"And yet?"

"And yet." Liam shrugged, at a loss as to why he was feeling the way he was.

"Do you need to go back to sea? We could go for a sail. I'll tell Grace it's an extended stag party. Head out for a week or so along the coast."

"In this weather? That does not sound fun."

"When have rough waters ever bugged you?"

"I must be getting old."

"Maybe you just need to get laid."

"Or that." Liam shrugged. "I haven't, ahh, sampled the goods here, so to speak."

"You're a smart man. Which is why I've hired you," Dylan observed.

"It wouldn't do to mess around in this town. The gossip chain is rampant. Everyone either knows or is related to one another. I don't want any sort of bad blood on my crew. I know when to keep it in my pants."

"Maybe you do need a trip abroad, just to change things up a bit. I've got a big project coming down the pipeline if you've an interest."

"How long would it be for?"

"Not sure yet. If anything, I wouldn't mind someone going to feel things out for me."

"Where is it?"

"Spain."

"Now that's interesting. I could spare a few weeks from the project."

"I'll keep you posted."

"You aren't just doing this to try and make me happy, are you?"

"No, it's a real project. The timing just works to break you out of your funk."

"It's not a funk."

"I know a funk when I see one."

"I've a mind to funk you right off this boat." Liam narrowed his eyes at Dylan and was rewarded with a booming laugh. Despite himself, he grinned.

That was what mates were for.

CHAPTER 8

*T*he rain didn't let up, which meant the lunch rush would be mad. There was something contrary about the villagers such that rain made them come to the pub in droves instead of staying home in the dry and warmth. Falling into an easy rhythm with Cait, Fi was already behind the bar and building pints when the door opened on a gust of wind.

Her head whipped up as a wave of longing and aware-ness washed through all of her senses, and she measured the man who stepped through the door in the seconds before his eyes landed on hers. It was like a lioness scenting her dinner on the wind. And oh, was Liam Mulder still a tasty morsel, Fi decided.

He'd grown even more handsome, if that was possible, and carried himself with that same easy confidence she'd first admired about him. He'd filled out even more since she'd last seen him, going from a lean man with muscles to a muscular man who looked like he used his hands for a living. Remembering what he could do with those hands made a flush rise to Fi's cheeks, and she dipped her head to check on the pints she was pouring to make sure she didn't overfill the glasses. Looking back up, she pasted a wide smile on her face and waited until Liam turned to her.

"Well, and look at this – it's a wayward pirate we've found wandering into our pub this stormy day," Fi said, winking at him cheerfully as she finished building the pints. Tamping down on the nerves that fluttered in her stomach, she moved to the end of the bar and placed the pints on a tray for the serving girl, then grabbed another ticket to start the next order.

"Fi? What are you doing here?" Liam asked, squeezing his way between Mr. Murphy and his cronies to lean his elbows on the bar.

"Well, where else would she be when she's in town? It's her mum's bar." Mr. Murphy slapped his leg and laughed, and Fi blew him a kiss.

"I could ask the same of yourself, Mr. Mulder," Fi said as she started the next round of pints. "It's more likely to find meself at this pub than you."

"Is Cait your mum?"

"Aye, I am." Cait came to stand by Fi and Liam looked between the two, his mouth dropping open.

"I should have guessed. You've a striking resemblance," Liam said.

"How's it you're knowing our Liam then?" Cait asked, and now it was Fi's turn to have her mouth to drop open.

"*Your* Liam? When did he become your Liam?"

"When he started building the community center with Dylan," Cait said with a shrug. "All right then, Connor, I see you want your whiskey. Stop giving me those puppy eyes. It'll be right along." Cait bustled off to the other end of the bar to fill orders, leaving Fi to deal with Liam.

"You know Dylan?"

"Aye, I do at that. Seeing as he's my best mate and my boss." Liam flashed her a grin and Mr. Murphy nodded soberly next to him.

"He's the lad who keeps everything together. They're turning my house into a community center, Fi. Can you believe it? It's what the space is meant to be used for. It'll be a happy home once again."

"That's right grand, isn't it, Mr. Murphy? Absolutely brilliant that they're using the space in such a manner. I know it's been a touch lonely for you since Maude passed on."

"That it has. She'd be pleased that her home will be filled with people once again."

Fi reached over and squeezed Mr. Murphy's leathery hand.

"Next round's on me."

"Why's that?"

"For being a good soul, that's why, Mr. Murphy."

"I'll join you on that round, if you've a mind to build a pint for me, Fi," Liam said, nodding gratefully when someone slid a stool toward him. Sitting down, he steepled his fingers under his chin and watched Fi with an unwavering gaze.

"See something you like?" Fi asked, a shiver running down the back of her neck at his gaze.

"Of course. A brilliant and beautiful woman building the most perfect pint of Guinness I've yet seen poured."

"Oh, he's a smooth talker now," Mr. Murphy chuckled.

"Don't let Cait hear you swooning after her girl. She'll have a boot up your arse so fast you won't know what hit you."

"Who am I booting now?" Cait demanded, skidding to a stop on her way to the cooler.

"Nobody that I know of," Mr. Murphy said, shaking his head as if to say he was just chattering nonsense.

"Mm-hmm," Cait said, singeing them both with a glare before stomping down the bar.

"Fearsome woman," Mr. Murphy decided.

"Thanks for saving me," Liam laughed.

"Lads first." Mr. Murphy shrugged a shoulder.

Fi chuckled, shaking her head at the two of them. "You two are trouble, aren't ya? Going to take on the town tonight?"

"In this weather? Goodness, no." Mr. Murphy glared at the rain outside. "I'll be staying right here, thank ye very much."

"As it pleases you, then. And you, Liam? We've a lovely Guinness stew on the menu today." Fi smiled at him again, going into full customer service mode, though her mind whirled at his presence. His very nearness was sending her nerves into overdrive and it was as if her body was hyperaware of what the man was capable of doing to her.

You're not some foolish young girl with no experience, Fi reminded herself. More than one man has brought a smile to your face in the bedroom.

But not like this man, her mind argued back.

Fi firmly shoved those thoughts deep down. Those types of thoughts ended in trouble, something she was distinctly not looking for on this trip – especially this close to home. She preferred having her dalliances and dating life kept far away from the gossips of Grace's Cove, and that was the truth of it. It wouldn't do to be seen flirting with the likes of Liam Mulder.

"That'd be great, Fi. It sounds like the perfect meal for a day like today."

"Same for me, pretty lady." Mr. Murphy nodded to her and Fi turned to tap the order into her mum's new computer. It had been quite a shock to everyone's system when Cait had finally upgraded to a digital drink and order register, and though it had taken months for everyone to be on board with the system, they'd eventually all agreed it was much more efficient.

Plus, it saved them shouting out menu orders over the music so often playing there. It was many a night that Fi had gone to bed with a throat too hoarse to speak for all the shouting she'd done.

"I suppose I should have connected you to here, what with you being related to Sean and all," Liam said when she turned back to face him again.

"I don't think we've ever really spoken of Grace's Cove, so there's no way you would have known. I'm just shocked to see you here, in my little village, after all these years. How's it been for you, then?" Fi cleaned glasses automatically as she spoke with him. The habit of tending a bar was ingrained in her and she was always moving, always doing something productive while she chatted.

"It's been good. I found my way into the company of my dreams. I get to travel the world. Meet wonderful people like himself here," Liam said, nodding to a beaming Mr. Murphy.

"How do you two know each other?" Mr. Murphy asked.

"Remember when I left uni and took my first job with Sean in Dublin? Liam worked on that project. He's a colleague of mine," Fi said, placing him firmly in the friend category. There would be no suppositions around their relationship if she could help it.

"Well, isn't that nice, then. Are you doing work for Dylan while you're here?" Mr. Murphy asked.

"Nope, though I'd love to come see the community center project one day. I'm here to plan Gracie's hen party," Fi said.

"Sure and we'll need to clear the streets for that one. The lot of you are terrifying together," Mr. Murphy said.

Fi let out a loud laugh. "You've been warned then."

"I'd be happy to show you the community center if you want to come by one day," Liam said, leaning back as the serving girl appeared at his shoulder with a tray of stew. Fi stepped away to get silverware and napkins, and by the time she'd returned, two steaming bowls of Guinness stew with some crusty brown bread sat in front of the men.

"I'd like that, thanks," Fi said, keeping it noncommittal. Turning, she grabbed another drink order – then stopped in her tracks.

Liam was Dylan's Liam.

The Liam Gracie had told her about.

The one who had gotten hurt in the cove.

The man Gracie had almost died healing.

The man of her dreams.

CHAPTER 9

"You didn't tell me Liam was *that* Liam," Fi said, bursting into Gracie's cottage without knocking. Not that she had ever knocked, nor was she likely do so in the future. Who needed to knock when there was a dog around to announce her presence? Bending automatically to where Rosie demanded cuddles, she looked up at Grace, who was standing by her long kitchen table, hands on hips, looking down at a pile of jars and creams.

"How was I to know Liam was 'that Liam' when you've never mentioned a Liam to me?" Grace asked, skewering her with a glare. "But now I'm offended that you didn't tell me you had a thing with this Liam, which you obviously did or you wouldn't be in such a fuss."

"I'm not in a fuss," Fi bit out.

"You come barreling through the door with barely a hello after months away, griping about Liam this and Liam that. I'm no rocket scientist but I do know when a woman's all aflutter about a man, there's been a situation in the past with said man. So now I'm the one who's offended that me own cousin and best friend hasn't told me about her time with this Liam."

"I swear I told you." Fi paused and thought back. Hadn't she told Grace? She usually told her everything.

"I'm not daft. I do remember what you tell me. I particularly enjoyed the French lover in the blue grotto –"

"Okay, okay, enough." Fi waved that away and stood, surveying her friend. "You look great."

"Thanks. Love will do that to a person, I suppose."

"No, I mean it. Really great. Your skin's all dewy and you look… rested. There isn't the same tension around your eyes."

"Sleeping through the night these days. Once I was with Dylan, the dreams dissipated. I can't tell you how refreshing it is not to wake up sobbing every morning."

"Oh, Grace, I'm so happy for you both. I know what an awful time that was for you." Fi moved across the room and enveloped her cousin in a hug.

"There, now I get a proper greeting. I'll put the kettle on. Seems we need to have a wee chat about this Liam of yours."

"He's your Liam. Well, Dylan's, anyway."

"I doubt Dylan knows Liam the way you've been knowing him – and if he has, we might be having to have ourselves a wee bit of a chat before I go and marry him."

"I didn't sleep with him," Fi said, plopping into the beautifully worn wooden rocking chair tucked in the corner by the stove, where it had sat now for sixty years.

"You were intimate with him." A voice over her ear made Fi jump from the chair and whirl around. Rosie danced at her feet and barked, delighted at the sudden movement.

"Fiona, you know better than to scare Fi like that." Grace made tsking noises as she brought the kettle and a basket of scones to the table. Fi glared at Fiona, for whom she was named, who hovered over the rocking chair. Grace had been the only one truly blessed with the ability to see Fiona once she'd passed on, but once in a while she'd made herself available to Fi as well. This appeared to be one of those times.

"Sure and my heart almost exploded out of me chest," Fi said, pointing a finger at the ghost. "You can't sneak up on a body like that."

"I wasn't sneaking. You sat on me," Fiona said.

"'Tis true. She was sitting there. You were in too much of a fuss to notice."

"How do you live with this woman?" Fi asked, crossing the room to sit at the table. Plopping her elbows on the table, she cradled her chin in her hand, staring balefully at the ghost across the cabin.

"She respects my space. For the most part. Plus, it's nice to have company out here. Dylan's gone much of the day or traveling, and I'm busy filling orders. She's an excellent resource when I struggle with some of my home remedies."

"How is Dylan?"

"He's lovely and a blessing and light to my life. Enough about him. Tell me about Liam."

"It's nothing."

"It's obviously something."

"No, I'm just making a big deal over nothing."

"Tell me."

"Forget it. Let's talk about your hen party."

"I will when you tell me about Liam."

"I'm being ridiculous. It was nothing. Just a night in passing years ago."

"You had a night together?" Grace set aside the cream she had been mixing and plunked herself down at the table across from Fi. "You most certainly did not tell me about this. I would have remembered. Liam is… well, let's just say if I didn't have Dylan, he'd be right up there on my list."

"Gracie!"

"It's true. He's a very handsome man," Fiona agreed. "I'd have given it a go in my time if my heart wasn't spoken for."

Fi buried her face in her palms. "Sure, that's a lovely image I just don't need right now," she griped.

"Women have needs. And those needs should be fulfilled by men like Liam. At least once in their lives," Fiona said, furthering Fi's chagrin.

"Great. Just great. My ghost of a relative has the hots for a man who pleasured me. Can this day get any weirder?"

"Ohhhhh, he pleasured you? I need details. Immediately. In full glory, at that." Grace's face lit up and Fi laughed.

"You are both weird, you know that?"

"We're all weird. We can hear people's thoughts, see ghosts, read auras, and perform magick. What in any way, shape, or form made you think we would be normal? That includes you, Fi, though I know you do your damnedest to ignore your goddess-given gifts. Gifts that came from my blood, if I must remind you."

"I don't ignore them. I just don't need them to live."

"Ignoring your power is not living."

"Listening in on people's thoughts isn't a fun life to live either. You have any idea how much shite you have to hear that you don't want to? It's a safety measure more than anything."

Grace reached across the table and squeezed Fi's hand.

"I know. I don't envy you that trait. At least not all the time. I can think of times it would come in right handy, though."

"Sure, it can. But I really have worked to shield it. If I don't, I'd never be surprised in me life. Oh! Speaking of surprises – and today has been quite the day for them – my parents gifted me a house. A house on the boulevard by the water. Me own house. Can you even believe it? They must be getting dotty with old age. Who gives someone such a gift?" Fi wondered aloud, then spilled her tea when Grace jumped up screaming.

"You're moving back! That's fantastic news!"

"Oh, calm down. I didn't say I was moving back. It's a place to store me things, is all. Now who's making the fuss? Calm down, woman," Fi said, grabbing a dish towel to mop up her tea.

"Still, it will make it more permanent. You'll come back more if you have something to tend to here. Oh, but I've missed you, Fi. I know you have a fierce wanderlust in you, I understand that. But I've missed you."

"I've missed you too," Fi said, "but I'm not settling down here. I'll be renting out the unit below and giving the money to my parents. I can't just accept a gift like that."

"I can understand where that would be hard for you. But you have to know it was done out of love. You never let them help you."

"It's important to me that I can stand on me own."

"You've proven that now, haven't you? No reason not to accept a gift like that at this point. It would be different if you were just out of uni accepting gifts of that nature. But you've gone out and proven yourself and your ability to provide for yourself. You have to let the people who love you do something for you once in a while."

"This is a big something," Fi said. She'd always been uncomfortable with receiving gifts, though she loved to give them.

"And you say, *yes, thank you, I love you*. Let your parents give you their gift of love," Fiona admonished from across the room.

"I did, and I do. But love doesn't have to be tangible gifts. Or a house."

"It's Shane's way of showing love. He knows it will be a property that can be a nest egg for you for life. Don't be difficult," Fiona said.

"I'm not…" Fi hunched her shoulders under Fiona's glare. "Yes, Fiona. I hear you."

"Now, back to Liam." Grace broke off a piece of cranberry scone and buttered it. "You know he's the Liam I saved."

"I do *now*. I wish I had known the connection sooner. It's right terrible what happened to him at the cove."

"He took a risk. That's his nature. Luckily, he believes

in magick and all things mystical, so you won't have that working against you two."

"There is no… it's not 'us two.' It's just… it was one night." Fi threw up her hands.

"A night you still haven't told us about," Grace reminded her.

"It's really nothing," Fi said. Then she sighed and launched into the full details of her night with Liam in Croatia, leaving nothing out. Once she was done, she waited while Grace studied her.

"You never called him."

"Why would I? It was a one-night thing. He was broken-hearted. I was moving to another country. It doesn't matter."

"It's rude."

"Oh please, it's not rude. There was no expectation of anything. You don't have to call if you don't want a relationship."

"But you said you were his friend first. You took him out on a mate's night. Mates would call."

"She's right," Fiona chimed in.

Fi jumped, having forgotten the old woman was there for a moment. "Since when does a woman owe a man a call after he chooses to please her? Isn't she allowed to take her pleasure and leave? She owes him nothing. How many times do men do this and women just accept it?"

"But he was being nice by leaving a note. He was treating you with respect and being a friend. You could have just sent him a breezy text checking in or something. Maybe saying thanks for a good night, hope to see you down the road – you know, putting him back in the friend zone but still being polite."

"I think she was worried about the fact that he threatened her carefully curated lifestyle," Fiona observed.

Fi got up. "Okay, I've had enough. I'll catch up with you later, Gracie. We can talk hen party stuff tomorrow. I need to go."

"Oh, Fi, don't go off in a huff."

"I'm not in a huff. I'm just done speaking on this. And I have things to do. Important things." Fi breezed out of the house, right into a wall of rain, and ran to her car. Knowing she was being impossibly childish, but not particularly caring, she turned her car toward town.

CHAPTER 10

*H*e could feel her body under his hands.

Still. After all these years, it was as though Fi had imprinted on his brain and he couldn't rid himself of her essence. She was a study in contrasts, lean limbs and sharp cheekbones, with a lusty laugh that could spear straight to a man's gut. She wasn't overtly feminine, not like the women he usually went for, but something about her reluctance to embrace the flowery womanly ways made her all the more sensual and appealing to him. Her slim jeans and loose button-down shirt seemed like a casual afterthought, and it made him want to unbutton her shirt slowly, revealing the smooth curve of her breast to him, and trail his lips over her skin like he'd done once before.

If only he hadn't been in his cups that night, he was certain he could have remembered even more details that now eluded him.

Fi had ducked out shortly after seeing him – something about a hen party and seeing Grace – but her cheeks were flushed, and she'd been quick to make her goodbyes. Liam liked when her cheeks tinged pink; it reminded him of her curled in bed, sated beneath him. Shifting uncomfortably on his stool, he tuned back into what Mr. Murphy was saying.

"Sure and that's a sad loss for Cork in the hurling this weekend," Liam quickly agreed, catching on that Mr. Murphy had wound his way back to sports. The old man had a routine to his conversations. It started with weather, moved on to politics, and finished with sports. After that, he'd be ready to take in any local gossip and add any tidbits of his own. Liam had learned more about how the village of Grace's Cove was run by patiently sitting down with Mr. Murphy than he had at any of the board meetings with the village council.

"What's my girl to you?" Cait startled him from the conversation, having snuck up behind him like a cat. She jammed her finger into his ribs.

"Hey!" Liam jerked away, shooting Cait a disgruntled look. "Damn, that finger is like steel."

"Next time it'll be a knife if you're hurting my girl."

"She's a vicious one, Cait is," Mr. Murphy nodded, sipping his Guinness. "I've seen her make Theodore O'Flanagan crawl out of here – all sixteen stone of him."

"He deserved it, that he did, Mr. Murphy."

"Never said he didn't. But a wee lass like yourself should have trouble handling a man of his size."

"Pssh, he's a pussycat." Cait waved that away and turned to focus on Liam. "You didn't answer the question."

"I didn't want to interrupt this lovely discussion,"

Liam said, turning to take a sip from his own pint and collect himself.

"Are you avoiding me, Liam Mulder?"

"I am not. I'm just enjoying this fine beverage your lovely establishment has provided for me today."

"Listen to the man. Evading the question," Cait said.

"It does seem so, Cait. Perhaps you should let the man to his peace then. It's hard to enjoy a pint with the hens pecking at you," Mr. Murphy said, then winced when he saw Cait's face. It was enough to make Liam laugh, for he didn't think he'd ever seen the pub owner so flummoxed before. Emotions warred on her face – from wanting to clock Mr. Murphy on the head to wanting to give him leeway because he was pushing ninety and had been her most loyal customer.

"It's a rare man who can get away with speaking such to me," Cait decided, though Liam saw her fists ball at her sides.

"Cait, I'll intervene before you tell dear Mr. Murphy here why he's been a bit sexist in his comments."

"Have I?" Mr. Murphy sat back and pulled at the newsboy cap he'd forgotten to take off. "Well now, I suppose that's something I should apologize for. I understand it's important to pay more attention to these things nowadays. I didn't realize how on trend I was."

Liam wasn't sure if condescending remarks could be considered 'on trend,' but seeing as how the old man looked apologetic, he decided to let Cait handle this one.

"No woman wants to be made to feel like she's just pestering a man while he's having a drink. I have a valid interest in Liam's stake in my girl, so I've a right to ask. Whether he's having a pint or not," Cait said.

"She's speaking the truth, Liam." Mr. Murphy wisely threw Liam to the wolves. "What's our Fi to you then?"

Lovely, now he had the two of them teaming up against him. If he didn't nip this in the bud, the whole village would be sniffing about in hours.

"I met Fi years ago when I was working on a contract for Sean up in Dublin. She came in as the translator."

"Her first job," Cait said, narrowing her eyes as she thought back.

"Aye, so it appears. I thought she was lovely and invited her for a drink." Liam held up his hand as Cait shifted an assessing look at him. "That was back before I knew not to mix business and pleasure. Also, I didn't know the familial relationship with Sean. He informed me and I canceled the date."

"Smart man," Cait murmured.

"I ran into Fi once again in Croatia – oh, say maybe seven or so years ago? I'd just had my heart broken and she was a friendly face. Not surprisingly, being your daughter and all, she sized up my situation quickly. She decided I needed a night out with mates to get me over my ex-girl-friend, poured a bottle of whiskey down my throat, and took me to kick my arse at pool. All in all, it was exactly what I needed to move forward. I was going to propose, you know."

That stopped Cait from whatever she was about to ask next, as shock crossed her face.

"To Fi?" Mr. Murphy asked, slapping the bar with enthusiasm.

"No, not that she isn't a worthy partner, I'm sure," Liam laughed. "To my ex-girlfriend. I had a ring and everything."

"What happened?" Cait asked, derailed from her line of questioning about Fi – exactly what Liam had hoped for.

"Well, let me tell you a story about two Russian women who are good at playing the long game."

By the time he'd finished, Cait was buying him another beer and all questions about Fi were forgotten. It was the best Liam could do in a town whose currency was gossip, and he figured that so long as Fi kept her mouth shut, their story should read as just friends.

Even though he wanted more.

Surprised at the thought, Liam glanced down at his pint – the third one, now – and wondered if the drink was getting to his head. It was a rare day he drank in the afternoon, but the project was running smoothly and he'd earned an afternoon off. Even so, he signaled to the other barmaid for a glass of water and settled back, mulling over thoughts of his past.

His feelings for his ex-girlfriend had been true, as was the shame that came after, when he'd discovered what a sucker he'd been. It had taken him a long time to trust women after that, and it would have been a horrible time for him and Fi to become more serious. Not that she'd called him, which still stung to this day. Liam wasn't sure why it bothered him so. The entire reason he'd slipped out early in the morning was to avoid any awkwardness and give them both the option of making sure there were no attempts at deeper attachment. He had asked her to call, hadn't he?

Maybe it had been a token gesture at the time, to show he was being a nice guy... but for some reason that hadn't taken the sting out of Fi's silence. For days after, he'd found himself glancing at his phone, wondering after her. He'd had too much pride to call Sean and ask for her number; no, that wouldn't have done at all. From what he could find, she wasn't on social media – or if she was, her accounts were locked up tight – and after a time he'd let her drift into the past.

From Croatia, he'd taken on several jobs across Europe, working himself to sheer exhaustion to escape the thoughts of his past. Eventually he moved forward, as one is meant to do after heartbreak, and now he could look back on that time with gratitude for having dodged a bullet. The experience had burned, but Liam had made a conscious decision to be even more generous and kind with his lovers. He enjoyed women, found them endlessly fascinating, and treated them with utmost respect. Never shying away from flavor or diversity, he'd worked his way through different countries, entertaining hordes of women, all of whom to this day would speak highly of him and fondly remember their time together. A user he was not. But love... well, that was a different story. No one had come close to working their way into his heart since.

It was... interesting that the reappearance of Fi in his life now irked him so, Liam decided, draining his pint and ignoring the glass of water. It was unusual for Liam to feel disconcerted when it came to women, but she crept her way into his thoughts more often than he would like.

Doing what he always did when he was troubled, Liam paid his tab and set off for a ramble. Fresh air and the open sea always cleared his head.

And it appeared that Fi needed to be quickly and staunchly removed from his mind.

CHAPTER 11

Fi wasn't sure if the rain matched her mood or if her mood had called the rain. It wasn't the first time she'd wondered if the extra magick she carried could call to the elements like that. Grace – well, they all knew when Gracie was in a snit, for the skies positively pummeled them and the seas would rage. But it had never quite manifested in that way for Fi, though now she wondered if she just hadn't been paying that much attention.

It was a particular trait of hers, ignoring what was right in front of her eyes. She'd grown up in a world of magick, hadn't she? It wasn't like she was completely immune to the mystical worlds that blended with reality in Grace's Cove. It would be impossible not to see – not to acknowledge – all the power surrounding her. Things flying across the room when Aislinn didn't want to pick them up, magick and spells and auras – it was all a bit much after a while. She'd learned to tune it out the best she could, and live a relatively normal life.

Grace thought she was crazy.

Why would you turn your back on your gifts? It was a constant lament of Grace's, for she considered her magick an added bonus to her life, and was legitimately shocked that Fi wouldn't want to delve further into hers. Grace had eventually let up on Fi, allowing her to live her life as she saw fit. From time to time she made comments, but for the most part Grace let Fi be Fi, and Fi let Grace be Grace.

It didn't help that Fi considered her traits to be some of the worst. Who wanted to be able to hear people's thoughts, let alone have dreams of the future? As a child, it had driven her all but mental and had caused no shortage of tough situations until Cait had been able to teach her how to shield herself from unwanted images and thoughts. She'd been a surly child until then – and rightly so, Fi mused as she turned her car down the lane. Who wanted to get flashes of Mr. Murphy having an argument with his wife or a man eyeing up her mother and thinking naughty things? It was right uncomfortable. Cait, and Fiona, had finally been able to get through to her and teach her how to enact mental shields so she could live her life unperturbed by others' thoughts.

Seeing auras and dream premonitions were another thing altogether. Grace thought she should be tapping into her dreams more – as in, using them to help see the future. But for what, Fi wondered as she took the winding cliff lane at a snail's pace toward the village. It wasn't like she needed to know the future. In a lot of respects, not knowing the future was what made life so exciting.

And she did crave excitement. Never one for sitting still, Fi had raced through life, always on the move and on to something different. Perhaps it was being around so much magick that made Fi expect life to always be interesting and amazing? Either way, she'd never craved marriage or babies or anything that might keep her in one place. She'd been off like a rocket as soon as university had let out and hadn't stayed in one spot since.

Drumming her fingers on the steering wheel, she considered what that meant, now that she would actually have a responsibility tying her to one spot. Being a homeowner was something Fi hadn't really envisioned, at least not for many more years, and certainly not in Grace's Cove. The gift from her father had quite thrown her. Yet, for some reason, it made her happy. Maybe there was something to be said for setting down some roots. Half a root maybe. One foot rooted and the other one lifted. She pictured a tree lifting a giant root-covered foot from the ground and giggled. Maybe she needed to work on her metaphors.

In any case, she was interested. Interested in decorating her new space, interested in being a landlord, interested in taking the art and curiosities she'd stashed away from all over the world and scattering them across her place. *Her place.* It did feel nice to think that.

Then, as if today hadn't had enough shocks, Liam Mulder had waltzed back into her life like he owned the town. That was something she wasn't quite sure how to react to. Perhaps she should have taken more time to think it through before racing off to Grace's cottage. Now she'd have both Fiona and Grace all over her when it came to Liam.

Speaking of Liam… Grace peered through the windshield

to see the man himself stalking down the lane as if he didn't even notice the sheets of rain that pummeled him. Sighing, she pulled the car up alongside him and rolled down the window.

"Having a nice stroll, are you?" Fi shouted over the rain.

"It's a lovely day for it." His teeth flashed white in his face and Fi's stomach did a funny little bounce.

"Would you like a ride?"

"I'll get your car wet."

"There's a wool blanket in the back. Hold on." Fi reached over and pulled a thick old blanket over the front seat. "Go on then, rain's getting in the window."

"I just fancied a walk to clear me head," Liam grumbled, rivulets of water streaming down his face.

"Oh? And what does your head need clearing of?" Fi asked. She had pulled the car back out onto the road and toward town before realizing she had no idea where Liam was staying.

"You."

Fi's foot hit the brake and Liam slapped his palm on the dashboard before quickly securing the safety belt over his shoulder and shooting her a look.

"Don't give me that look. You can't say stuff like that and not expect me to react."

"Did you want me to lie then?"

"No, I don't want you to lie.But you can't say...*that*... and not expect a reaction."

"What's driven *you* out into the rain?" Liam asked, ignoring her comment.

Fi glanced at him to see a heated look in his eyes.

"Hmmm," she said, putting her eyes firmly back on the road instead of on the man who suddenly seemed to fill the car with his presence. His nearness was making her... something, Fi thought, and firmly steered her mind away from where those thoughts wanted to go.

"Hmmm, she says. And here I thought you were the honest sort, Fi," Liam said, his voice husky.

"I went to see Grace," Fi said, dancing around his question. It wasn't a lie, and she could live with that.

"You left the pub in a bit of a hurry."

"Sure, and I didn't want to get stuck with the lunch rush. I'm not on the till there, you know."

"I suspect you'd work any shift your mum asked of you."

"Where am I taking you, Liam?" Fi asked, approaching a small roundabout in the center of town.

"Where do you want to go, Fi?"

"Are you purposely being difficult?"

"Do you find me difficult? Interesting."

"Is it?"

"You know what else I find interesting?"

"I'm sure I can live without knowing," Fi ground out. She continued to drive, taking a right on a whim since he'd given her no destination.

"I find it interesting that you didn't answer my question. I also find it interesting that you think I'm being difficult. I find it interesting that your cheeks flush a particular shade of pink when I'm around."

"They most certainly do not," Fi exclaimed, shooting a quick glare at Liam.

"Oh, they most certainly do. Particularly after I've had my mouth on you," Liam said.

Fi let out a little yelp. "Must you bring that up?"

"Of course. It's a memory I'm quite fond of."

"Great – is this where you need me to thank you for your services? Build your ego up and tell you what a stud you are?"

"It certainly wouldn't hurt," Liam decided.

Despite her discomfort, Fi laughed. "Thank you for your services, good sir."

"You're welcome," Liam said.

"Where am I taking you?"

"Why don't we go for a drive?"

"Because I have things to do."

"Like what?"

"Like fix things at this new building my dad has insanely gifted me. There's loads of projects. I'm busy, Liam."

"Projects, did you say? I'm a project manager, you know."

"And I'm sure you're well paid. Which is where you should be. Managing your projects."

"I took the day off."

"Must be nice your boss doesn't fire you."

"He trusts me."

"That's grand for you and all… but seriously, where am I taking you?"

"To look at your projects. I like projects. Let me help, Fi."

"I don't need help. I need to be away from you," Fi

burst out. A smile stretched wide on Liam's face. "Oh, don't look like the cat who ate the canary."

"I'm not. Just wondering why you can't be around me. I thought we were mates."

"Mates don't do… what we did."

"Sure they do. If they're good mates," Liam decided.

"Liam."

"Fi."

"Where am I taking you?"

"I told you."

"Goddess save me from stubborn men," Fi griped and turned the car toward her new flat.

CHAPTER 12

"It's got good bones," Liam said, standing in the middle of what Fi already considered 'her' flat. He turned in a circle. "And it's fairly updated. What are you thinking you'd like to see done here?"

"I'm not sure yet. I only found out about it this morning." Fi tried desperately to ignore the sensations that slipped through her at the sight of him filling her living space. He was a large man, all muscle and brawn, and his presence dominated her senses.

"And you said it was a gift? Hell of a gift."

"Here, let me get you a towel. If there are even towels here," Fi amended, noticing he was dripping on her floors. She found a linen closet in the hallway and breathed a sigh of relief to see that it was stocked with towels. Pulling a few out, she returned to Liam, who thankfully hadn't moved, and handed them over.

"Mind if I take some of this wet stuff off?"

"Sure, um – we can hang your coat in the bathroom or in the little mudroom in the foyer." Fi's mouth dropped open when Liam unbuckled his belt. "Wait, no, what are you doing?"

"I can't exactly give you tips on your projects if I'm walking around in dripping wet clothes," Liam pointed out, divesting himself of everything but his boxer briefs before Fi could protest.

"Liam! You can't be naked in here."

"I'm not naked," he pointed out.

Stalking past him, Fi drew the curtains on the front window lest anyone pass by and see an almost-naked Liam Mulder in her window.

"What am I supposed to do with you now?"

"Does the flat have a dryer?"

"I have no idea."

"Well, let's have a look."

With that, Liam ambled over to the kitchen, opened a door she hadn't seen before, and discovered a small washer and dryer tucked away inside.

"That's convenient," Fi said.

"It is. We'll just pop my clothes in for a quick spin and we can talk about your projects. So, tell me, why such a big gift?"

Liam turned and Fi forced herself to drag her eyes up from the tiny towel that barely hugged his waist. She met his eyes.

"What?"

"The gift. This house." Amusement lit Liam's eyes and a smile hovered on his lips.

"Stop it. I can't deal with you being naked right now."

"I'm not naked."

"You might as well be."

"Is that an offer?"

"No!" Fi said and shot off across the room to stand by the window, drawing in small gulps of air. This man should not have the effect he was having on her. It was likely only because it had been a while since she'd had any sort of... relations. That must be it, Fi decided; she was just in a dry spell.

"Too bad." Liam smiled again and wandered back into her living space, forcing Fi to draw a deep breath. She hated feeling out of control and needed to turn the tables on this – and fast.

"Okay, fine. Sure, it's an offer. Obviously, we both have an itch to scratch." She almost choked at the look on Liam's face – from arousal to instant panic.

"Sure and that's a lovely way to phrase it, Fi. Is this what you want? Just to scratch an itch?"

"It's obvious that's what's bugging us. We have unfinished business. Might as well be getting it out of our systems now." Fi sauntered closer to Liam until she stood just in front of him and trailed a finger down his chest.

"You've a lovely way with words, Fi. *Really* seductive." He caught her hand before it could trail any lower, and Fi was amused to see annoyance flash across his face.

"I'm quite the siren, I am," Fi looked up at him and bit her lower lip. "Shall we test out these beds?"

"Stop it. Why are you being like this?" Liam gave her a gentle shove backward.

"What? You don't like it when I meet you where you're at? I'm just offering up what you're going after." Fi shrugged, stepping closer again.

"I wasn't going after sex."

"I find that hard to believe."

"Maybe it was the end game, but not my starting point."

"Then what are you doing, Liam? Why are you coming here and getting in my space, throwing around all these heavy looks and sexy flirtations?"

"Because you bother me, I like you, and I'm interested in finding out why that is."

Fi bit back what she was about to say and just looked at him – really looked at him. His face was a mixture of frustration and arousal, and something else she couldn't put her finger on. Despite her best efforts, the faint colors of his aura began to shine around him, which meant that her defenses were low. Before long, she'd start reading his thoughts.

"You need to go. Now," Fi decided, stepping around him and stomping over to the dryer. She pulled out his still-soggy clothes and dumped them in his arms.

"You're throwing me out?"

"Yes, now. You need to go," Fi said, desperation kicking up in her stomach as she realized how on edge she was. It wouldn't do to read his thoughts – no, not this man – and if he stayed a moment longer, she would be invading his privacy. Unable to explain that to him, she pointed to the door.

"Like that? You're tossing me out. I tell you I like you and you're throwing me out?"

"Correct."

"Moments ago you were offering to bed me."

"I'm a complicated woman, Liam."

"I'll say. You can't really be throwing me out in my underwear."

"Nobody lives here. You can dress in the hallway."

"Fi... talk to me." Liam stood by the door, his eyes warm and measuring on hers.

"I have nothing to say. Just go, please," Fi said.

"I don't like leaving you like this."

"We're mates. I'm not mad. But I do need you to leave. I don't feel well." Fi stepped back as concern filled Liam's eyes and he moved forward.

"Can I do anything?"

"No, it's... I had a curry for lunch. Stomach issues. Best you leave," Fi said as mortification stained her face pink.

"Ah, I've been there. I'll go. But we need to talk about this," Liam said, stepping out in the hallway.

"Maybe, maybe not. It's really not much of a thing at all. Truly. Okay, off with you then. Safe home," Fi said, closing the door and bolting it before racing to a bedroom and throwing herself on the bed face down. Embarrassment flooded her, along with something else she couldn't quite put a finger on – shame, perhaps? She'd all but thrown herself at the man, then tossed him from her flat. Not that he hadn't been pushing her buttons, Fi reminded herself as she flipped over to stare at the ceiling. What with him prowling around almost naked and being all... *Liam* in her face. He had to know the effect he had on her.

Or did he? She hadn't really told him, had she?

This was why she didn't do relationships, Fi reminded herself. Dating and flirting were not her strong areas. She always ended up being unable to shield her gift from the person she was close to, and she had been treated to some very uncomfortable revelations. Like the time she'd accidently discovered her lover was working her around to bringing another woman into their bedroom. And maybe something about golden showers? She'd left that one behind as fast as she could. There were some things best left undiscovered, and some fantasies best left unsaid.

Fi's gift often put her in an awkward spot, much like this moment, where she'd tried to take control of a situation and had it backfire in her face.

"I had to tell the man I'd had a curry..." Fi groaned and covered her face. "Now that's all he'll think about when he sees me."

CHAPTER 13

"*A*re you sure you're wanting to get married then?" Liam asked Dylan, causing the other man to stop writing in his notebook and glance over at him from across the table. Liam had crashed the ship's galley once again – it served as their temporary office, and was close enough to Fi's apartment that he hadn't soaked up too much more rain.

"Aye, I'm sure," Dylan said, leaning back to study Liam.

"Women are mental," Liam said, stretching his legs out in the sweatpants he'd found stashed in one of the rooms.

"They are at that," Dylan agreed. Reading his friend's mood right, he reached behind himself to open a small cupboard door and pull out a bottle of whiskey.

"A wee dram then?"

"Why not?" Liam shrugged, crossing his arms over his chest as his mind whirled with what had just happened. They'd gone from teasing and playful to almost angry in mere moments. There was something else going on there, but Liam hadn't been given the chance to dig deeper. He didn't like puzzles – well, he liked finishing puzzles. It was more that he didn't like unanswered questions, and Liam had a lot of them for Fi.

"Why not, indeed? The weather certainly calls for it," Dylan said, his tone placid as he poured them both a small measure of whiskey. "Slainté."

"Pissing down out there," Liam commented.

"Indeed. Are you here to talk about the weather or talk me out of marriage?"

"Neither. I just wanted to know why you're tying yourself to a woman forever, is all."

"You've met Grace. You love Grace."

"Aye, that I do. She's a powerhouse, and she saved me life. I'm forever indebted to her. I'd marry her if you didn't."

"And yet he questions marriage." Dylan looked up to the ceiling and shook his head.

"I'm just trying to understand women."

"It'll take more than an afternoon and a bottle of whiskey for that particular endeavor," Dylan said, a smile flitting across his face.

"You don't think you'll get sick of Grace?"

"No. There's times where I want to throttle her, and her me, so we step outside and take some space. But it only needs a bit to calm down before you remember why you love each other. Plus, she's magick. In all the ways. My life with her will never be dull and for that, I'm eternally grateful."

"I suppose that's a blessing. You're right – it's going to

be a fascinating dance the two of you lead in the upcoming years."

"And I welcome every dip and twirl of it. So, tell me, Liam – is it Fi?"

"Why would you say that?"

"Just an inkling," Dylan said with a shrug.

Liam groaned, running his palm over his face before downing his whiskey in one gulp. The heat trailed down his throat, warming his belly, and making him wish that something else was warming him.

"It's been something like four hours since I've seen her. How could the gossips possibly be spreading the news already?"

"I only need one gossip," Dylan reminded him, reaching over and pouring another dram for Liam.

"Of course – Gracie. She would know. What did she say?" Liam demanded.

Both of Dylan's eyebrows rose. "Well, color me surprised, my good lad. I had no idea we'd be sitting down talking about 'he said, she said' this afternoon. You're never one for gossip."

"That isn't entirely true, as you well know. I like to keep my ear to the ground."

"Sure you do, on projects and feeling the pulse of the villagers' responses to things. But you've never been one to settle in for women's gossip."

"Also untrue. I love women. I let them gossip around me all the time."

"And pay them barely a lick of attention when they do. Go on then, tell me what's bothering you."

"Ach, man, you're doing me head in. Yes, it's Fi. We have a history," Liam said.

"Ah, the plot thickens."

"Aye, it does. A night in Croatia. Nothing too serious, but she was there for me to help me past my breakup. I like her. She's whip-smart and unsure of herself at the same time. There's something about her that... I don't know. She's a puzzle for me to figure out."

"She intrigues you."

"She does. And I don't know why. She's not my typical type."

"A lovely lass though. You could do far worse. I owe her a great debt."

"Why's that?" Liam cocked his head at Dylan.

"She was instrumental in making sure I got to Gracie. Remember when I went and tracked her down at a friend's place in Italy? Fi was the friend. She reached out to me. Smart woman."

"She is smart. And funny, and one of the lads, and yet not."

"You like her."

"I told you I did, didn't I?"

"Calm down, I'm just trying to clarify things. What's got you in a snit then?"

"She threw me out of her apartment. One moment we were flirting" – Liam decided to leave out the part where Fi had offered him a quick shag – "and the next she was tossing me out. I can't understand it. And she wouldn't talk to me or tell me why." He also decided to leave out the bit about Fi's upset stomach. It wouldn't do to embarrass the lass further.

"Hmmm," Dylan said, and turned to pull a packet of crisps out of the cupboard. They both reached for a handful, quietly crunching as they considered the situation. "What do you want?"

"I want to know why she bothers me so much."

"I hope you didn't say that to her like that."

Liam paused, then said, "I don't think I did."

"So, maybe you romance her? You know women, despite your protestations that you do not. Just do your thing and she'll be dating you in no time. But if you hurt her, I'll have to kill you."

"See? This is exactly why I *don't* want to date her. You can't date someone in this town without everyone having a say in it. Christ, we even had a bet going on about when you and Gracie would end up together."

"And I'm guessing you thought that was fun?" Dylan smiled, and plucked another crisp from the bag.

"When it's not me, it's grand fun."

"My suggestion is, if you're confused at the moment, then don't start something you can't finish. I know, I know" – Dylan held up his hands at Liam's look – "that sounds ridiculous. There's no way of knowing what your end game with Fi could be. I just mean, treat her carefully. If you don't think you could see yourself with her for a longer haul than your usual stints, then keep her as a friend. No reason not to be nice to her."

"I don't know what I see for us. Nothing, really, seeing as she just chucked me from her apartment."

"Then you've received your marching orders. Respect that. Be her friend and ease off a bit. She'll let you know if she's interested."

"Play the waiting game?"

"Why not? We're here for a while anyway. Now, tell me, what apartment was Fi in? Does she have a place here now?"

Despite his protestations about gossiping, Liam settled in to tell Dylan the news while the boat rocked gently beneath them and the rain buffeted the hull. Moments like this always reminded him of the bonds made with his mates at sea, for there was no finer companionship than riding through storms with friends.

CHAPTER 14

*S*he was in the cove, that much Fi knew immediately, sitting cross-legged in the sand and staring out at the water. A pack of tarot cards lay at her feet, and she seemed to be giving herself a reading. Shuffling, Fi stared out at the water and considered her question.

"Show me the future," Fi said, and laid out a card.

If this had been real, and not a dream, Fi would have been able to say that tarot cards weren't meant to be used for such open-ended questions. But, seeing as how she was dragged deep into her subconscious for this particular storyline, all she could do was watch from afar and see how it played out.

The first card indicated indecision and a splitting of paths. Fi wanted to break through the dream and point out that, of course, that was how the future worked. People had choices. The next card indicated travel and exploration. Fi flashed to an image of herself, ten years from now, sipping a glass of wine on a balcony in Ecuador, admiring the bustling streets below her. Fi studied herself, looking for clues of what would come, and what she saw in her face made her... sad, she realized. From the outside, this Fi looked content. World-traveled, well-dressed, confident, and successful. But the lines around her eyes and the tension in her mouth indicated sadness. She was lonely, Fi realized. The scene switched, pulling her back to the beach where she flipped another card, indicating another path.

This one held Liam. Of course it did, Fi thought in annoyance; he was all she'd thought about all day before finally tumbling into sleep. But the scene didn't change this time. Instead, she glanced up from her spot, nestled in the sand, to see him strolling across the beach toward her, a smile on his face. The wind tousled his hair, and Fi jumped up, joy racing across her face as she held out her hands to him. When a flash of blue light shimmered in the cove, Fi forced herself to pull out of the dream – all the way out, until she lay blinking at the ceiling of her new apartment, her heart racing, her brow damp with sweat.

"That's not fair," Fi said out loud, looking up at the crown molding that cornered the room. She'd fallen asleep with the small light on the bedside table still on, and now she pulled herself up to sit, leaning back against the headboard and drawing deep breaths to calm herself down.

It wasn't often that she had these dreams, for she'd done her best to train herself out of them. That training – and a sleeping pill on occasion – helped to blanket her from these moments.

They'd started when she was quite young, and had been quite a surprise to everyone. At the tender age of three, Fi had woken to tell Cait that Mr. O'Sullivan's barn was on fire. Luckily, Cait had accepted the mysteries of Grace's Cove enough at this point to suspend disbelief and ring over to Mr. O'Sullivan's house, waking a very annoyed household. Their annoyance had turned to gratitude when they'd been able to discover the fire and stop it before it did much damage or hurt their livestock. Since that day, Cait had paid close attention to her daughter's dreams, and Fi had tried to suppress them as best she could. It wasn't a formally known trait of hers around the village, yet whispers followed her. It had singled her out for being different at a young age, and combined with her ability to read thoughts, she was well aware of what people weren't saying to her face.

Having Grace as an ally had proven to be the best thing for her; they were not only family, but genuinely liked each other. Where Grace embraced her magick and ran roughshod over her family, Fi had quietly tried to suppress hers and lead a normal life. Irrespective of their different approaches to their gifts, the girls had always been thick as thieves, and that had helped to combat any loneliness that would otherwise have occurred when the other children shied away from them. It helped, too, that Grace was startlingly beautiful and dynamic – a force to be reckoned with. She was born to be popular, and pulled Fi along in her wake.

As the years went by, Fi stopped talking about the dreams unless they were something that absolutely needed attending to. If anyone was in grave danger – like when David had fallen from a cliff and broken his leg with nobody about to see – then Fi made sure to help. But other things? Less subtle dreams? She left well enough alone regarding those. It wouldn't do for her to tell Mr. Flanagan that his wife might be enjoying the company of the local doctor. Or to announce that Susan at school had a crush on the new boy from Derry. As far as Fi was concerned, that was meddling. One thing she did believe was that no one could know the ramifications of intervening in situations like that, and Fi didn't feel the need to have the weight of that on her head.

Now, with tonight's dream, she found herself deeply annoyed. Did she *ask* what her future looked like? No, she hadn't. Fi didn't need or want those answers. What she wanted was to have a good night's rest, enjoy her friend's hen party, and catch up with her family. Liam was not in her plans.

For a moment, because it was almost three in the morning, according to a quick check of her phone, she let herself think about Liam walking across the sand to her. Her dream self had looked happy – truly happy – and that was something she hadn't ever really felt, Fi realized. Was that the missing piece of her puzzle? Love? A man?

Shaking her head in frustration, Fi took another deep breath and studied her manicure. It wasn't fair to think she couldn't be happy on her own. She loved her life, genuinely enjoyed her work, and was fascinated by traveling. She refused to believe that a man would be the final key to her happiness. There had to be something else bothering her, Fi mused, and then groaned out loud when it came to her.

"Is this one of those life lessons where I need to accept all aspects of myself in order to be happy?" Fi asked the crown molding. When it didn't respond – because, duh, it was an inanimate object – Fi glared at it.

"So you're saying I'll be happy with Liam, but not happy following my path – a path I dearly love?"

Still no response.

"I hate these dreams," Fi decided. Rolling over, she flicked off the light, pulling a pillow over her head for good measure.

CHAPTER 15

"*O*h, this is going to be fun." Keelin, Grace's mum, clapped her hands when she entered Gallagher's Pub, followed by the rest of their inner sanctum of friends and family. For the first time in ages, Gallagher's Pub had closed to the public to become the unofficial 'Hen Party Headquarters' for the day and night. Keelin and Flynn's farmstead had been commandeered by the men for a day of Highland-style games and copious amounts of whiskey. With strict assurances that they would stay put, the women had felt comfortable taking over the village for their party.

Fi called out a welcome from where she was helping the team of makeup and hair stylists arrange their tools on two long tables she'd pulled out from the back room. Cait had found an old dressing rack from some dusty storage closet and Fi had hung all the dresses she'd selected on it. Maybe she'd gone overboard, Fi thought, eyeing the rack that exploded with tulle and satin, but better to have too many options than not enough.

She wasn't particularly looking forward to one part of

the night: Grace had requested they do something to honor all their extra-special gifts. Knowing Grace, she was probably thinking something along the lines of calling upon the goddesses while they danced naked through a stone circle. If that was what she wanted, she should have picked a different maid of honor, Fi thought as she smiled at the women who poured in after Keelin. Each one was equally as luminous as the next, and they all had a special place in Fi's heart. For a moment, she paused and studied them all as they chattered and hugged each other just inside the door, talking a mile a minute over each other, acting as if they hadn't seen each other in years.

She missed them, Fi realized. As much as she traveled, Grace's Cove and the people in it were still her home and her heart. Making a mental note to schedule more trips home, she moved forward to greet the group.

"Aislinn, I've missed you," Fi said. She was enveloped in a cloud of rose-scented body oil as Aislinn hugged her close, the bracelets dripping from her wrists tinkling softly together. Pulling back, Aislinn shook back her wild mane of hair, now threaded with grey, and studied Fi's eyes.

"You've sorrow to you. What's going on?" Aislinn demanded.

"Would you hush? Today is about Grace," Fi hissed, pushing her away and shooting her a warning look as Keelin squealed and threw her arms around Fi.

"We'll talk later," Aislinn said, and continued into the pub.

"Talk about what?" Keelin said and looked from Fi to Aislinn. Narrowing her eyes, she looked more closely at Fi. "What's going on with you?"

Taking a deep breath, Fi looked to the ceiling and counted to three. Goddess save her from meddling family, she thought, and pasted a smile on her face.

"Nothing at all, Keelin. Just Aislinn being nosy. You look lovely," Fi said, and not just as a distraction technique. Keelin had aged well, her curvy body just as generous as it had always been, her strawberry-blond hair only highlighted by the brilliant white strands that now joined it. She'd braided her hair back from her face, leaving the rest to tumble down her back, and though lines now etched her lovely face, in Fi's estimation they only served to make her more beautiful. Keelin had been like a second mother to her, and every year she grew more stunning.

"You'll not be able to keep secrets from this bunch, as you well know," Keelin reminded her. "When you're ready, you come tell me what's bugging you."

"What's wrong?" Morgan asked from behind Keelin's back and Fi bit back a groan. Morgan – a knockout beauty from the day she was born, from what Fi could tell – looked nervously over Keelin's shoulder.

"Morgan, lovely to see you. It's been a while. How was your trip to the States?"

"Oh, it was so much fun. We did all the tourist stuff that I've been wanting to do my whole life! We went to Times Square in New York and the Golden Gate Bridge in San Francisco. I'm so glad we took this trip."

"I can't believe you traveled in a van for three months. Together. And didn't kill each other," Fi said, grabbing onto any conversation that would steer the watchful eyes of her aunties away from asking too many probing questions.

"Well, I'll say we had our moments. But Patrick – well, he's good at smoothing my moods by now, you know. Oh, there's Kira. I haven't seen her since she finished up her masters. Kira!" Morgan called Aislinn's daughter over to them.

"Kira! It's been, what, like three years?" Fi asked, holding her friend for an extra-long hug.

"Well, if you weren't so busy traveling all the time, maybe you'd bother to visit us once in a while." Kira, a strong mix of mystical and pragmatic, wore her hair long and her heels high, and had a sharp mind for business. Under Morgan and Aislinn's tutelage, she'd become a wildly successful photographer, had rocketed both her mother's galleries and her own work into successful world-renowned businesses, and now divided her time between Grace's Cove and traveling.

"Like you're one to talk," Fi said. "Weren't you just in Nairobi?"

"South Africa, actually," Kira said. "Things are well?"

"As can be. Kira, you look fantastic," Fi said, admiring Kira's outfit. She wore slim leather pants paired with combat boots and a wispy lavender lace shirt, and her hair was left messy and tumbling down her shoulders. One feather earring hung from a delicate silver chain at her ear, and mixed metallic necklaces clamored for space at her neck. She should have looked ridiculous, and yet it all worked for Kira.

"Thanks, as do you. Though you look…" Kira trailed off at Fi's glare.

"If one more of you tries to read my aura or whatever, I'm going to scream."

"I don't need to read your aura to know you look tired. Those dark circles under your eyes will tell me just fine." Kira nodded to Fi's face. "You're lucky you've a makeup team to do you up nice, or you'd look haggard in the pictures."

"Did I say I missed you? I think I forgot what a bitch you are," Fi said.

"I thought that was what you liked about me," Kira said, her grin spreading a mile wide in her lovely face.

"Remains to be determined," Fi muttered, then laughed when Kira poked her in the ribs.

"Ladies," Cait called from the bar, "I've got mimosas. Today is going to be a long day, so remember – water between drinks. And food all day."

"She's speaking like we aren't Irish," Grace said, squeezing between Fi and Kira. "This isn't our first bit of craic."

"No, but you know Cait loves driving the train. Might as well let her," Kira said, turning and hugging Grace close. Despite her mood, Fi's heart warmed and she threw her arms around her girls. She'd missed these two. So many of her memories included the both of them. It was nice being around people who really knew her. That was the one thing about traveling all the time – she was constantly meeting new people, and had to fill in her back-story. In some respects it was nice, because Fi could always control the narrative and be someone new if she wanted to be. But in other respects, it was lonely. There was nothing like spending time in the company of people who knew her through and through.

"What's up with you?" Grace demanded, turning to look at Fi's face.

Scratch that thought. Fi rolled her eyes and turned away. "I swear, if one more person asks me that…"

"Asks you what?" Cait popped up at Fi's elbow and Fi looked around desperately for a mimosa.

"I think it's definitely time for alcohol," she muttered. Ignoring her mum, she went to the bar and grabbed a mimosa. Taking a few quick sips, she let her nerves settle as she looked out at the group.

They'd kept it small, for Grace wasn't one for huge crowds anyway, and the group consisted of their nearest and dearest: Keelin, Margaret, Cait, Aislinn, Morgan, and Kira. The only person missing was Fiona, and Fi raised a glass to her.

"I'm here. You know that," Fiona barked out from over Fi's shoulder.

Fi almost dropped her drink. "Damn it, Fiona. You should be knowing better than to sneak up on a body like that," she griped, turning to glare at her.

"If you'd stop blocking your power so much you'd have seen I've been here the whole time," Fiona said, smiling warmly out at the group of women who had descended upon the hair and makeup stylists. Grace circled the rack of dresses and turned with her hands on her hips to look at Fi in question. When she saw Fiona, she bounced over to the bar and took a mimosa in her hand.

"Fiona! You're here."

"Of course I'm here. Once the stylists are gone, I'll

make myself more known to the group. For now, just know I'm always here with you. Today should be a fun and powerful day for you all. When women come together to celebrate love, it's magickal."

"It is, isn't it?" Grace sighed, tipping her glass to take a sip. "I hadn't thought I'd be sentimental about all this, but I can't help it. I'm so happy and I just want everyone to feel this way."

"Not everyone gets their love. You're lucky," Fiona pointed out. "Some people never let themselves see what's right in front of them and miss their chance."

"Yes, some people do," Grace said, slanting a look at Fi.

"All right then, everyone!" Fi pushed away from the bar, clapping her hands to get everyone's attention. "The theme for the hen party tonight is going to be Un-Bridaled. You get to choose a ridiculous bridal gown to wear all night and yes, we will have games. Feel free to choose from any dress on the rack; I bought a ton in different options as I didn't know what you would like. Pick your favorite and then let the makeup team work their magic."

Squeals greeted her announcement as the women attacked the rack. Fi choked back a laugh as Gracie launched herself into the thick of it, loudly declaring that she was meant to get the worst dress of all.

"Can we just let today be about Grace?" Fi turned to Fiona.

"For now, yes. You've a good heart, Fi. Listen to it."

CHAPTER 16

"*M*ay I just say, you all look…" Fi struggled to find the appropriate word.

"Like a bridal cake?" Aislinn twirled in her ruffled explosion of organza and satin. She resembled a cupcake or a cockatiel, Fi couldn't decide.

"Like a hooker?" Keelin struck a pose in her body-hugging sequin and lace number, which was just a shade past slutty into indecent.

"Like I should be in an eighties music video?" Kira asked, admiring her huge shoulder-padded stuffed sleeves on her ruffled dress.

"Like a doily?" Cait asked, looking down at her lace hoop skirt in bewilderment.

"Like Madonna?" Gracie said, voguing around the room in her white leather, lace, and pearl dress. How Fi had been lucky enough to find such a dress, where no fabric or embellishment was scorned, was beyond her, but she'd known instantly that Gracie would love it.

"Like I'm waiting for my long-lost lover to come back from war?" Morgan asked, twirling in her dress, which did indeed look like a cross between a milkmaid's uniform and a ghostly apparition staring out to the water.

"Like I'm the last girl at the ball?" Margaret asked, twirling in her princess gown with horrific pink ruffles and tucks cascading across the wide skirt.

"And you... Fi. Goddess above, but I think you look like a dominatrix," Gracie decided and then let out a peal of laughter at Cait's horrified look.

"She's not far wrong," Kira whispered.

Fi choked back a laugh as she looked down at her "gown." Made primarily from white latex, it hugged every inch of her body, making her look wet and shiny. Then the intrepid designer had decided to add crisscrossing ribbons of pearls to all of the dress, and fluttery lace sleeves. A part of Fi enjoyed rocking such a dress, as she'd normally never be caught dead in something like this.

"It's a look, that's for sure," Fi commented.

"And how do I look?" Fiona asked, materializing in front of the women now that the hair and makeup people were gone. The women turned as one, shouting their appreciation as Fiona twirled in a slinky satin number. Keelin and Margaret hugged each other, a sheen of tears in their eyes, as they smiled at Fiona. Fi knew it wasn't often they got to "see" her – that particular gift fell to Gracie. For years, Gracie had acted as translator for the family, filling them in on any necessary messages from Fiona. But in moments like this, being able to physically see Fiona again was astounding.

"Who knew you'd finally show up in my bar and be a trollop? I should've guessed that about you," Cait teased, though Fi knew her mum well enough to know she was just as affected by Fiona's presence as the rest of the group.

"Well, if I can't have a little fun now that I don't have to worry about my reputation..." Fiona shrugged.

"I don't think you ever really cared about your reputation to begin with," Margaret said.

"True enough. What a boring life I would have lived if I'd spent my time worrying over others' opinions."

"Now that everyone is here," Fi said, bringing the attention back to her, "it's time for our first game. I have a little scavenger hunt planned."

The women cheered.

"After that, we'll meet in Aislinn's backyard for part two of the evening. Part three will reconvene back here at ten p.m."

"What's part two?" Gracie demanded.

"You'll find out when you get there," Fi said.

"And three?"

"If I didn't tell you two, why would I tell you three?"

"You're an odd sort; who's to say?"

"Since when am I odd?"

"You've always been odd."

"Says the woman who calls on storms when she's in a bad mood and hunkers in her cottage muttering spells all day," Fi said, and laughed when Gracie made a motion as though to cast magick over her.

"Be careful, or I'll be mixing up a particular brew just for ye," Gracie warned.

"That is terrifying." Fi turned. "Okay, ladies, here are your tasks. Let's see what you can accomplish. You can do this in teams, on your own, or as a whole."

"Oh, let's go as a whole. It'll be more fun that way," Morgan said.

Fi refrained from pointing out that they wouldn't be able to determine a winner if they went as a group. This was Gracie's party; she could choose.

"Grace?"

"A whole. Much more fun."

"As a whole it is then," Fi said, and turned to the door. "And there are no rules. You may use all tools and power at your disposal."

"Ohhhh, game on," Gracie cheered.

"First up, steal a kiss from Mr. Murphy."

"Oh, that's not a challenge." Kira rolled her eyes. "He kisses everyone."

"You have to find him first," Fi said.

"Oh, you've gone and hidden Mr. Murphy," Cait laughed.

"What else is on the list?" Gracie grabbed it from Fi's hand, laughing as she read, "Guess the number of condoms in the jar. Where's the jar? Hmmm, persuade Mrs. Culligan to give us all free scones. That's going to be a tough one – that woman is tighter than Fi's dress."

"I'll take care of Mrs. Culligan. Many a time she's had a free pint in here," Cait said.

"Dance down Main Street and get three wolf whistles." Grace laughed, and Fi snatched the sheet back from her.

"That's enough. Onward, ladies, onward," Fi cheered.

They poured out of the pub in an explosion of lace and

ruffles, and headed toward the little downtown in hopes of finding Mr. Murphy.

"This is really lovely, Fi. You've done a good job here," Cait said, falling into step beside Fi.

"Thanks, Mum. I think she'll have fun tonight."

"She already is. Just look at her." Cait nodded to where Gracie was dancing in front of one of the café windows, much to the delight of the patrons inside.

"Do you want to talk about what's bothering you? Did you have another dream?" Cait asked, as they slowly followed the group bounding down the road ahead of them.

"I did, yes, but it's something I need to figure out on my own."

"Is it? You know I'm always here," Cait said, squeezing Fi's arm.

"I know you are. And I'm ever so grateful for you. It's just… complicated."

"Liam," Cait said, and it wasn't a question.

"No. Yes… maybe not. I don't know. Maybe him. Maybe your gift of the apartment building. Maybe just looking at my life," Fi said.

"You know I'm not one to meddle," Cait began, and Fi shot her a look. "Fine. I meddle sometimes. But in this, I'll step back. I can't speak about what's going on with you and Liam unless you tell me what's in your heart. For now, I'll say, give yourself some space to grow."

"What do you mean?"

"You always hold yourself to this rigid view of what your life is supposed to be like. Anything that makes you veer from that path gets kicked away. I admire your tenacity, but I also think you might want to take a more flexible approach to your future. You can't know what it holds."

"Well, I kind of can. Sometimes, at least." Fi squeezed the bridge of her nose as the dream flashed before her eyes again.

"Predicting the future doesn't mean one particular way is your future, Fi. We all have choices. You can change your path at any time," Cait reminded her.

"And if my predications show me several futures?"

"You choose your path based on all the information at your disposal."

"That's what I'm afraid of," Fi sighed.

"Stop lagging! I've found Mr. Murphy. He's hiding in the back of Mary Margaret's deli. Let's get him, ladies!" Gracie screeched, and a crowd of satin and lace went running.

"Let's go!" Cait grabbed Fi's arm and together they raced down the street in time to see Gracie dip Mr. Murphy in an Oscar-worthy kiss. The old man's cheeks bloomed an alarming shade of red, and the entire group of women cheered.

"I think that's the first proper kiss he's had in years," Cait decided, coming to a halt as she shook her head at the spectacle.

"Sure and it's a lovely kiss," Mr. Murphy said.

"Such a great kiss, I think it makes me want to dance," Gracie said.. Hooking arms with Fi, she pulled her into the mix as they all began to boogie their way down the high street.

It was a vision the town talked about for years – the day traffic came to a halt as the magickal women of Grace's Cove took to the streets and, for a moment, time stopped as the women danced their hearts out.

CHAPTER 17

"*I* had no idea you could kick so high. And in that dress," Keelin laughed at Margaret as they all piled into Aislinn's backyard. The scavenger hunt was complete, and much to everyone's delight, Fi declared them all winners. Grace's Cove had ground to a halt as the women terrorized it in their ridiculous bridal gowns, and Fi was certain the pictures would haunt them for years.

"I still have some moves, I'll have you know," Margaret said, doing a sassy little cha-cha-cha step as she made her way to where Fi had set up round two of the party.

"What's your plan now, Fi? We all sit in a circle and sing songs?" Gracie giggled.

Fi had laid out a large picnic blanket in Aislinn's garden, and set cushions in a circle. Fairy lights twinkled in ropes above them – thankfully, no rain had ruined their outdoor excursions yet. Fi doubted that even the elements would dare to betray Gracie on one of her big days.

"Something like that," Fi said, stopping to pick up a

small package she'd placed on the table. "Everyone, pick a cushion and settle in." The women, still laughing from their exploits, dropped to the cushions in relief.

"There's an extra cushion," Kira said, pointing.

"That's Fiona's cushion," Fi explained. She could just see her presence outlined there, wavering – but her color was pure and everyone knew she was near.

"Now, to the serious portion of our night," Fi said.

"Uh oh. I don't have to be walking through fire and the like, do I?"

"No, that's for the fun portion of the night," Fi teased, and Grace grinned at her.

"In all seriousness – and because I know this will matter to you, Gracie – all of us have come together to give you a gift that we hope you know holds all of our love for you."

Touched, Grace held a hand to her heart and looked around at the circle of women who beamed back at her. Fi leaned over and gave her the small box, and Grace carefully unwrapped the silvery paper, sighing in joy at the bracelet she found there. Handcrafted from silver, each stone in the bracelet represented a woman of their circle, and each had their own attribute. Rose quartz for Keelin and her mother's love for Grace. Agate for Morgan, representing courage. And so on, all the way down to Fi's stone – a sapphire for curiosity.

"This is brilliant," Gracie said, running her hands over the bracelet. "It's really powerful, and I can feel how much love is pouring through these."

"It'll help, you know, in your healing and your tonics,"

Keelin said – she had always had an affinity for stones. "It should channel your energy through love."

"I can feel that."

"We'll also add an extra touch of, um, oomph, I suppose," Fi said, tripping over her words. This was the part she'd felt really uncomfortable with, but Keelin and Aislinn had insisted. "As a circle, now, we'll pour our energy into blessing the bracelet. Fiona is here, and she'll add her love as well."

There – she'd lightly danced around the words 'magick' or 'power' by using 'energy.' Love was energy, right? Decidedly uncomfortable, she glanced to Keelin, who registered the look on her face and smoothly took over.

"From here, I'd like to put the bracelet in the middle of the circle and for all of us to hold hands." Keelin waited as the women dutifully held hands, and all closed their eyes. Fi looked around for a moment, studying the serenity on each woman's face, before closing her eyes. A warm hum began to vibrate through her core, like she had plugged herself into an electrical socket, and the feeling of it had her popping her eyes open again as Keelin began to speak.

"We invite the circle to be ever open, yet always unbroken. May the love of the goddess bless this bracelet and be always in your heart. Nine women, nine stones, nine powers contain. Merry meet and merry part, and merry meet again."

Fi's eyes widened as a flash – the blue of the deepest water of the cove – hovered above the bracelet for an instant before winking from sight. She blinked, looking around the circle to see everyone else smiling and content. How were these women so at ease with the magick they created? It was something that had never sat easily with Fi, and now once again she was forced to contend with it. It was hard to ignore what was directly in front of her face.

"I can't believe you allowed magick at my hen party." Gracie laughed at Fi's face as she picked up the bracelet and secured it on her wrist. It sparkled there like it was lit from within, and all the women nodded their approval.

"It is your party, after all. It wouldn't be right if I didn't include… well, what makes you *you*," Fi said, shifting uncomfortably in her latex dress and wishing she'd made a different choice for her outfit.

"And you, too. When you're ready to accept it," Gracie said, and Fi shifted again as all eyes turned to her.

"It's not that I'm not accepting it, and that's the truth of it. It's just not a comfortable thing for me. You've taken it like a duck to water, you have, Gracie. Since the moment you could walk you've been all fire and magick. But that's not me." Fi shrugged a shoulder.

"You don't have to live like Grace to accept your power," Aislinn said softly.

"I do accept it. I just don't want to rely on it or use it to live."

"Is that what you think we do? Use it as a crutch to prop our lives up?" Keelin asked, raising an eyebrow at her.

Fi realized she might be offending her family. "No, I don't think that at all. I envy your ease with what you have. I'm just… I guess I've always needed to prove I can do it on my own. Without any added… abilities."

"But those abilities *are* you. You wouldn't tell a rugby

player not to use his muscles in a match. Or a singer not to use her voice. It's just part of who you are," Morgan said.

"I… yes, I suppose," Fi said, hating that the attention was on her once again. Seeing her distress, Gracie came to the rescue.

"Enough about Fi. This is my night, ladies! I believe there was a round three?"

"There is! At the pub. Shall we?" Fi jumped up, grateful to be leaving that particular discussion behind.

"They'll not let this go, you know," Kira whispered at her shoulder.

"As long as they lay off tonight, I can handle them," Fi said back.

"Then let's party and I'll steer them away if I see you cornered."

"Hopefully it'll be too loud for them to do any talking anyway," Fi grinned.

CHAPTER 18

"It's a club!" Grace crowed when they piled through the door of Gallagher's Pub again.

"It's a pub club," Kira amended.

"The closest I could get to a dance club in Grace's Cove." Fi smiled and winked at Cait, who had been just as eager to help transform the pub into a swanky nightclub for the evening. They'd put Shane and a few of the other local lads to work all day while they were out, and now the pub barely resembled its usual charm. Instead, black velvet had been draped over the walls, hiding the Guinness adverts and whiskey signs, and a real disco ball had been hung in the middle of the ceiling. In the corner, a shiny DJ booth was set up and all the windows were covered in the same black velvet. Tall mirrored tables had been set at various points around the room, and twinkle lights and small candles completed the look. The only thing that remained the same was the long length of the polished bar that had always dominated Gallagher's Pub.

The DJ at the booth straightened and flashed the ladies

a disarming grin before starting up "Girls Just Wanna Have Fun."

"Yes!" Aislinn shrieked and threw her hands in the air, shimmying her way across the... well, what was now the dance floor of Gallagher's Pub.

"Oh my." Fi bit back a laugh.

"Whiskey," Grace decided, turning and looking imploringly at Fi. "We need all the whiskey."

"I'm on it," Fi said. She caught Cait's eye and they moved as one, mother and daughter's movements so in sync that they barely missed a beat as they ducked under the bar, pulled out trays, glasses, and shot glasses. Because, of course, there would be shots.

"Champagne as well?" Cait asked, brandishing a bottle she'd pulled from the glass cooler behind the bar.

"Yes. I don't know that I can see Margaret taking down a shot of whiskey."

"Then you don't know Margaret," Cait laughed. "But yes, she'll likely drink a nice glass of red or some champagne instead."

"This is great. Look how much fun she's having." Fi smiled and leaned on the bar, looking out to the middle of the dance floor where Grace had thrown herself with more enthusiasm than actual grace.

"Oh, here's the others." Cait nodded to the door and the cheers in the room grew as the rest of the women in the village piled through the door. Fi had thought it would be nice to invite everyone – it was a small town and with Gracie living here full-time, she didn't want to exclude people. She'd designed the day to have some fun with the smaller, more intimate group of friends, and then the rest of the village could come party. She had spread word of the theme, and now Fi almost lost herself laughing at the mix of ridiculous bridal dresses walking through the door.

"Would you look at Meredith? I swear her dress is so awful she looks beautiful," Cait laughed, looking at the local baker who was done up in a gingham wedding gown. There were veils, trains, sparkles, and hair piled high on heads. It was like a fabric and makeup store had exploded in the room, and Fi could not stop laughing.

"This turned out to be way funnier than I was expecting," Fi admitted.

"Go on now, get out there with your friends then. I can cover this bar with me eyes closed. I've got backup coming in just a wee bit – don't you give me that look, Fi," Cait warned, deflecting Fi's protest at her mother working on such a special night. But, knowing Cait, she would work all night. That was where she was happiest, Fi thought as she sashayed out onto the dance floor with a tray full of shots for everyone.

"Ladies! Let the evening begin," Fi called, and the women surrounded her.

Hours later, everything had become a bit blurry. They had danced – oh, had they danced, Fi thought, chuckling softly to herself as she leaned against the bar. She had finally stepped breathlessly off the dance floor to seek out a glass of water. She wasn't sure when the last time she'd danced was, Fi realized, let alone for hours on end while a DJ played on. Now, nearing one in the morning, Fi was astounded to see Margaret leap her way into the middle of the circle and start a nifty Irish step dance. Where had she learned that?

Fi gulped down her glass of water eagerly, the cool liquid calming her breaths, and filled it once more. Then, moving around the side of the bar, Fi leaned against it to watch the dancers.

When the door blew open, almost slamming against the wall with a loud crash, Fi jumped and her mouth dropped open. Frozen, she watched as Dylan's stag party poured through the door with raucous cheers, coming to claim the women.

Liam's eyes locked on hers, and Fi froze as everything inside her turned to warm liquid heat.

CHAPTER 19

*W*hat was she wearing?

The sight of Fi dressed in shiny latex that hugged every dip and curve of her slender body, and made her look like a dominatrix angel, had Liam pulling up short. Every thought in his brain seemed to tie up into one big knot, and his nerves went haywire, as his entire focus narrowed to Fi. He didn't see the room, the other people, or anything other than this woman – his woman – standing against the bar, her luminous eyes wide in her face.

When she licked her lips, Liam's vision clouded and he started toward his woman.

"Hey there, mate, slow it down." Dylan blocked his trajectory across the room and grabbed him by the shoulders. "I know what you're about to do, but I'll remind you her family is here."

Shaking his head to clear the blind lust that clouded his brain, Liam narrowed his gaze to meet Dylan's.

"Don't look at me like that. I'm saying no."

"Shouldn't you be in your drink enough by now to not talk reason to me?" Liam hissed.

"I am. But even I can see this is a bad idea. You can't throw her over your shoulder and leave. Not like this. Not this late. And definitely not when she's dressed like that."

"She looks…"

"Yes, like a wet dream. Which is why you'll be treating her with nothing but respect. Or I'll be taking you out of here myself. Understood?"

"I…" Liam took a shaky breath, and then another. "Aye, mate. Understood."

"That's a good lad. Now, be a gentleman and offer to buy her a drink."

"How am I supposed to talk to her when she looks like that?"

"Don't look down. Look at her face. The dress is… well, yeah, we can discuss that another time. I have my own bride to try and avoid manhandling." Dylan shot a glance over to where Grace beckoned to him from the dance floor.

"You're far too reasonable at such a late hour on your stag party."

"Get me some whiskey then, lad. It's gonna be a long night, I'm thinking," Dylan laughed. He slapped Liam on the shoulder, certain the crisis was averted, and went to greet his bride on the dance floor. Cheers filled the room as they embraced, and despite where his head was at, Liam smiled after them.

They'd had a long day of festivities, and for some reason it seemed the more Dylan drank, the more sober he became. Liam, along with the rest of the lads who had spent the day out at Flynn's participating in Highland-style games and a cookout accompanied by a massive bonfire, all staggered around the room in various stages of drunkenness. Liam prided himself on being able to handle his drink, but he was decidedly not sober.

Nor was Fi, by the looks of it, he thought as he approached her. She still stood at the bar, watching him. Schooling himself to keep his eyes on her face as he drew closer, he tried a bright smile in her direction.

"Oh, that's himself three sheets to the wind, isn't it then?" Fi laughed, then slapped a hand over her mouth when she hiccupped.

"Would this be the time to point out pot and kettle being black?" Liam asked, leaning against the bar.

"Sure and I'm a bit wobbly, I'll admit it," Fi sniffed, sticking her nose in the air and then breaking down into a laugh. "But that's what hen parties are for, are they not? And what makes you think your stag party can go and interrupt my well-planned hen party?"

"We missed our womenfolk," Liam said with a shrug.

"Bah, that's a lie. You men always gripe about your women and how we talk too much. Now you want to be by us?"

"Sure. We do think you talk too much. But we'd be lost without you," Liam said. He raised an eyebrow at Fi's look. "What's that look for?"

"Why, Liam. It sounds like you positively respect women."

"I do respect women. They make the world go 'round. They are fire and ice, strength and beauty, and manhood would die out into a cold and unforgiving place without

women to right our ships. You're the captains, the naviga-
tors, and the backbone of humanity. I adore and respect
women, absolutely."

"And yet we talk too much."

"Nobody can be perfect, darling, though you're damn
close to it," Liam admitted, not caring that his filter wasn't
in place this evening.

"Am I now? Why's that?"

"You're fiery, and yet unsure of yourself. You're brilliant, but not posh about it. I like how courageous you are
– going after what you want and traveling the world alone.
Not many people could do that. You know how to listen, to
be a friend; you can hang with the boys and yet be utterly
and completely feminine when need be. You're the perfect
package, and I'm doing my damnedest not to look at you
in this dress and think inappropriate thoughts right now."

"Damn it, Liam. You confuse me. You reject a tumble
with me and yet say these things to me now. After how
many whiskeys?"

"It's the way men work, darling. We're complicated
beings."

"Not that complicated," Fi grumbled.

Liam watched as she tugged at the latex bust of her
dress. Groaning, he looked away.

"Would you stop fidgeting? I'm trying not to look at
the dress."

"What's wrong with the dress?"

"There is nothing wrong with the dress. You are every
man's fantasy in the dress. I'm trying to be respectful of
you, but you're wearing a fantasy outfit and it's taken me
brain in a decidedly naughty direction. This is not your

fault; I am but a humble man with a very vivid imagination."

"Is that right? And what are you imagining, Liam?" Fi asked, licking her lips once again.

Liam's blood soared in his veins. "Nope. Not going there. I see your mum. And there's your father. Don't try my patience, Fi. You're not being fair."

"I suspect you're right, though I'm tempted to play with you a bit more," Fi said.

Her words sent lust raging through Liam. Taking a step back, he held up his hands. "I'm going to dance with your mum. Or someone else. Anyone."

"Nice chatting with you, Liam." Fi beamed at him and gave a little waggle of her fingers before turning to bend across the bar and reach for a bottle of whiskey.

Liam's mouth went dry as he watched the latex stretch across her bum. Turning, he plunged wildly into the dancers, grabbing someone at random and twirling around, allowing the music to drum out the beat of lust in his head.

"Well done, lad," Dylan called as he bounced past Liam.

"I hate you for bringing me here," Liam shouted.

"Nah, you'll be fine. Drink up!" Dylan shoved a bottle of whiskey at him, one of many being passed through the crowd, and Dylan drank, not caring anymore what the night would bring, so long as he could drown out thoughts of Fi in that dress.

"Slainté, mate. This is going to be one hell of a wedding."

CHAPTER 20

*S*he'd switched to water. Probably for the best, Fi thought as she saw another woman make a fool of herself and throw herself into Liam's arms. Turning, she washed glasses out of habit and tidied behind the bar.

"This is the best party," Gracie gushed, leaning over the bar to smack a kiss on Fi's cheek. "Thank you so much for throwing it for me."

"It's the best I could do in our little village since you refused to let me whisk you away for a weekend in France."

"Bah." Gracie waved that away with one hand. "Who needs France? I've got everything I need right here."

"Do you?" Fi wondered, putting a glass down to lean her arms on the bar and look out at the dance floor where the DJ dutifully played on, though it was damn near three in the morning and people were dropping like flies.

"Of course. Do you see that?" Gracie gestured out to where Cait and Keelin swayed to a song together, and

Dylan paraded Aislinn in a sloppy circle around the dance floor. "That's love. All of them. Each powerfully unique, each magickal in their own right, and they're all right here. There's more excitement and magick in this roomful of people than in the whole world. Why do I need to leave to find that? My roots are here, yes, but so is so much beauty and wonder. I love living on the cliffs, and feeling the ocean's heartbeat in the cove, and watching my plants grow and become part of healing potions for the world. I'm content here, Fi. I don't need to race around the world to be happy."

"I envy you that," Fi sighed.

"You could have that. If you let yourself." Gracie nodded toward Liam.

"My happiness should not be tied to a man. What kind of woman would I be if that was so?"

"I'm not saying it should be tied to a man. Men aren't meant to be the answer to your happiness. But a partner – a good one – can enhance your life."

"I think I'm good." Fi shrugged.

"Are you? I wonder."

"Now is not the time to wax philosophical, my love," Fi said, gently putting her walls up.

"Ahh, if ever there was a time to get philosophical it's at three in the morning after a dram or three of whiskey. The witching hour, Fi – it brings out great truths."

"Drunks and children never lie," Fi agreed.

Grace threw back her head and laughed. "I love you, Fi. Now I'm going to take my man out of here. I trust you'll make sure Liam gets home safe?"

"Me? Why me? He's got friends here," Fi pouted.

"All of whom have women with other things on their mind."

Fi looked up to see various couples slipping from the pub, arms thrown around each other and whispering into each other's ears.

"Fine. I'll make sure Liam gets safely home."

"That's a good lass. Have I told you I loved you today?"

"You have. Many a time. I'm happy for you, Gracie. Dylan's a good man and I know you'll have a beautiful life together."

"Oh, and there's herself trying to make me shed a wee tear at this hour," Gracie said, squeezing Fi's arm before retreating across the room to throw her arms around Dylan. The pickings were slim on the dance floor, and aside from Liam, Margaret and Sean, and her mum and da, everyone had slipped out the door. The DJ let the last song play out and everyone looked up at the silence that blanketed the room.

"Go on, all of you. I swear if I see any of ye trying to clean up I won't come to Gracie's wedding," Cait threatened, switching into pub-owner mode and making shooing motions with her hands. Fi came around the bar to say her goodbyes and was shocked when her mum motioned her to the door. "You as well, Fi. Get on with ye."

"But this is my party. I'm supposed to clean up."

"Liam, you'll be seeing Fi gets home safely," Cait instructed Liam, who slanted one eye closed and grinned lopsidedly at her.

"This man? He's so pissed he can barely stand," Fi laughed.

"Then you've a duty to see him home. Go on then, Fi. You've a duty to our guests."

"Ye can't be serious right now. Kicking me out of me own pub at three in the morning?"

"I'll be reminding you the pub is mine, and you're lucky I let you tend to it." Cait pointed to the door. "Out."

"And I'll be reminding you of this the next time you're down a barmaid and call me for help," Fi groused as she stepped out the door with a humming Liam. Her mouth dropped open when the door slammed shut behind her. "Me own mum. Turning me out on the street with a drunken man. She's obviously not concerned for me safety."

"You're a fearsome woman, Fi. I wouldn't want to be meeting you in a dark alley. Unless you're wearing that dress and feeling amorous about me," Liam said, grabbing her arm and trying to swing her into a lopsided two-step.

"Oh, hold on, let's straighten you out then," Fi sighed, and tucked her arm through Liam's, tugging him down the street. Then she stopped, so suddenly that he almost bowled her over when he kept going. "I don't know where you live."

"It's... on a street." Liam squinted down the darkened street, turning in a full circle. "Hmm. One of these."

"Is that so? And which one of them is it?"

"One with a flat on it."

"And what does the building look like?"

"It has a blue door." Liam stopped, looked up at the

sky, and then at her again. "Damn, Fi, have I told you how delicious you look tonight? I want to just slurp you up like an ice cream cone."

"Ohhhkay, let's get you on then," Fi said, ignoring the shivers of lust that raced through her at his words. Her body definitely remembered being devoured by Liam's mouth, and every second had been a dream. Realizing she had no choice, Fi tugged his arm to direct him down the street toward the water and her apartment building. Liam hummed an incoherent song the whole way, and when they stopped in front of her door, he pulled her close.

"Hey!" Fi said.

"I didn't get to dance with you tonight. Dance with me, pretty Fi?"

"I… fine, Liam, I'll dance with you," Fi said, and allowed Liam to pull her close. He smelled of the sea, she realized, as she pressed against his body and nestled her face into his chest. Salt water and something more earthy – all male, though. Her heart fluttered in her chest as he sang to her, in Gaelic this time, and moved them in a slow dance under the wan light of the moon. The waves lapped gently at the shore, and Fi wrapped her arms around his neck, enjoying his warmth. For a moment, she let herself sway there in his arms and imagined coming home every night to him – this gentle giant of a man who could still respect her and make her feel safe even if he'd drunk an entire pub's worth of whiskey.

"Come on, Liam. Let's get you to bed," Fi said, pulling away before her heart made her do something silly, like telling him she wanted more. She tugged him upstairs.

The man was asleep before he hit the bed. Once she'd made sure he was comfortable, with a glass of water by his head, Fi peeled off her dress and put on a loose tank and sleep pants. Curling into her window seat, she watched the moonlight dance across the water and wondered just what it was she was searching for.

CHAPTER 21

Fi jolted awake when she was gathered into someone's arms. Confused, she pushed back and glanced around blurrily, trying to figure out where she was and what was happening.

"Shh, I'm just bringing you to bed," Liam whispered against her ear.

Fi blinked up at him as he cradled her close, bringing her down the hallway and depositing her on the bed. Her mouth dropped open when he crawled in next to her, pulled her to him, and tugged the blanket over the both of them. Wanting to protest, but also enjoying the comfort of his warmth, Fi allowed sleep to pull her under.

Hours later, Fi blinked awake once more, shocked to feel an arm tossed loosely around her waist. For a moment, she let herself lie there, enjoying the feel of a man in her bed, before she shifted and started to slip from under the sheets.

"Good morning... or should I say afternoon?" Liam snagged her wrist and tugged her back down.

"Is it that late already?" Fi asked, sitting stiffly on the side of the bed and refusing to lie back down with him. A part of her admitted he looked super cozy, and with the way her head felt right now, she'd love nothing more than to crawl back into bed and nestle in his arms. But because of that feeling, she lightly detached his hand. "I have to use the toilet. Would you like a coffee?"

"Tea, if you have it," Liam said, smiling at her in such a disarming way that Fi felt her stomach flutter. He looked adorable with his hair rumpled and eyes sleepy. At some point in the night he must have taken his shirt off, and her eyes trailed across the muscles of his chest, causing the flutter in her stomach to kick up a notch. Taking a deep breath, Fi skedaddled to the bathroom, reminding herself firmly that this man had recently rejected her advances and now was not the time to get *those* thoughts about him. She was determined to keep Liam in the friend zone, as she had promised herself to do the other night after she'd tossed him out of her flat. This wasn't the first time he had made her want more, but she didn't have the head or heart for playing games with a man. Never one to engage in manipulation or flirting tactics, Fi had always missed the greater subtleties that came with the dating game. Instead, she'd put it out there when she wanted to be with someone, and if they didn't feel the same, she moved on. Simple. It should be simple, Fi repeated to herself as she padded to the kitchen and put the kettle on. Why did things with Liam not feel simple?

"I went to the shops yesterday if you fancy a brekkie," Fi called down the hallway. Liam let out a raucous cheer, which she took for a yes, so she began pulling ingredients from the fridge. In moments she had the tomatoes cut and bacon on a tray for the oven. Popping the bread in the toaster, she poured beans into a pan on the stove and cracked eggs into a bowl. Humming, Fi prepared the tea, then poured the eggs into a pan, content with cooking. Though her mum had never been a great cook, her dad had enjoyed teaching her the basics in the kitchen. Between the two of them, Fi could mix a mean cocktail and serve a solid meal without breaking a sweat.

"How's your head then?" Fi asked when Liam appeared on the other side of her breakfast bar. She had decided to gloss over the fact that they'd just been snuggling in bed together.

"It's a bit fuzzy, but nothing I can't handle." Liam gratefully accepted the mug of tea she handed him.

"You were delightfully in your cups last night." Fi shot him a look.

"As were you, if I recall. Although all I can seem to focus on is you in that dress. Why must you play with a man's heart so?" Liam groused.

Fi chuckled. "I wasn't planning on seeing any men last night, it's your fault the lot of you showed up."

"And I'll be forever grateful to Dylan for making us go. The sight of you in that dress will be always burned into my brain. I don't guess you'd be wanting to put it back on for me while you serve me breakfast, will you?"

Fi slanted him a look.

"That's a no, then. Though I must say, you're looking as beautiful as ever in this lovely outfit as well. I can't think there's much you don't look gorgeous in, though I think this look is particularly special. Maybe because I don't think many men get to see it?" Liam pondered aloud.

Fi turned and put her hands on her hips. "What are you doing?"

"Me? I'm complimenting you."

"Why?"

"Well, why not? Can't I tell you that you look beautiful?"

"No, you can *not*."

"Why not? I thought all women enjoyed hearing compliments."

"They do. But you're… complicating things."

"How so? Honesty never complicates things." Liam took a sip of his tea and studied her over the mug, his eyes stormy in his face as he tried to figure her out.

"Because you've rejected me. *Again*, mind you, and that's told me all I need to know about where things are with us," Fi said, turning to stir the eggs and to check the bacon in the oven.

"I did not reject you because of what you're thinking. It just wasn't the right time."

"Well, the offer is off the table."

"Sure and women are finicky ones, aren't they?" Liam asked of no one in particular, raising his eyes to the ceiling and then bringing them back to Fi. "How is this fair to me? If I was pressuring you to have a shag, I'd be a lowlife male who only wanted one thing. But when you do it and *I* say no, then you'll not be interested in me at all? I hardly think that's fair, Fi."

She stared at him for a moment, caught by his words.

"Well, shite. When you say it like that, I guess I do sound like an arse, don't I?"

"It's just a double standard is all." Liam shrugged a shoulder.

"You're absolutely right, Liam. I'm sorry," Fi said, leaning over to touch his arm, meaning every word. "I would be mad at you if you ran hot and cold on me if I turned you down for sex. That's not right of me. For that I'm sorry. Can I offer you breakfast as an apology?"

"Ah, food. The way to me heart." Liam smiled his disarming smile, and Fi's heart flipped in her chest. Loading his plate and then hers, she rounded the breakfast bar and climbed onto the stool next to his. For a few moments, they ate in companionable silence, while Fi's brain worked through what was bugging her.

"I think then… all things considered… it's best if we are friends," Fi said, tentatively broaching the conversation.

"I've never stopped being your friend," Liam said, cutting into his baked tomato.

"I know. I just mean… that's it, just friends. It's probably best."

"How so?"

"Because you're here. I travel a lot. Long distance rarely works. All that. I like you, Liam. I always have. Best not to muck things up with a relationship," Fi said, feeling more confident as the words tumbled out.

"I travel a lot as well, Fi. We often travel to the same places. I suspect we would travel well together, if you allowed it."

"I'm sure we would. But… well, I think it's maybe too

complicated. We have a lot of overlapping friends and business partners. Don't you think it's best not to complicate things?" Fi turned, her eyes meeting his.

"No," Liam said simply, before turning back to his meal.

"Well, I'm not sure how to respond to that," Fi admitted, huffing out a laugh as she pushed her plate away and stood, carrying her mug to her window seat. The seat had already become her comfort zone and now, with the moody sky outside reflecting her inner turmoil, she sipped her tea and curled up to watch the water.

"Does everything always line up in a neat row in your life?" Liam asked, nudging her so she moved over on the seat. Though there was barely enough room for the both of them, Liam managed to wedge himself across from her so she could study the handsome edges to his face.

"Usually, yes," Fi admitted, turning away to scan the water once more. "I like being in control."

"And this makes you feel out of control?" Liam asked, gesturing with his mug to the two of them.

"There is no *this*," Fi grumbled.

Liam smiled, this time an almost feral smile that shot lust straight to her gut. "Come on, Fi. I never fancied you for a liar."

"Fine – obviously there's an attraction here. A basic, healthy lust. We're two attractive people. We have a bit of a history. That's normal. It's not a big deal," Fi said.

"Isn't it? What if I wanted it to be a big deal?"

"Well, you'll be having to look for that from another woman, Liam. I'm leaving the day after next for my next project. I won't likely be back here until the wedding." Fi had taken a project that she'd been offered two days ago. It had come as a bit of a surprise, but she'd felt like it was the right choice for her career. Luckily, if she could wrap things up quickly, she'd only be gone for a few weeks.

"I can wait," Liam decided.

"Can you? Because this is my life, Liam. One that I dearly love. I love traveling to different countries, often with little notice. I pack lightly, rarely stay long, and keep moving. It's important to me to explore the world."

"I'm a sailor, Fi. That's what I do."

"Aye, but I'm not. So we'll be exploring the world on our different paths," Fi said, and then softened when he just looked at her. "Listen, we're mates, okay? I like you, Liam. I really do. But I think it's more important to me that we stay friends than try something that might ruin our relationship. I won't deny an attraction, but I think it's best for all involved if we stay as just friends."

"I'll respect your decision, on one condition," Liam said, reaching out to play with her fingers.

"What's the condition?"

"If the time comes where you may think differently, you'll allow me to try and change your mind."

"Why? You could have any woman. Why are you after me?"

"Because you're not any woman, Fi. I can bide my time."

"That's not... that was not my intention for this conversation," Fi said, shooting a frustrated glance at Liam as he left the window seat and began to tidy the kitchen.

"That's fine. I'm excellent at negotiating, Fi. I know when to back off and when to push. You're not ready."

"I may never be ready. I may always just want to be friends," Fi all but shouted from across the room.

"That's fine with me too. But I suspect I'll be changing your mind at some point."

"This is not... Liam. No. You can't put that out there. It'll just make things weird."

"You're the only one making things weird. We're friends. I've got it." Liam held up his hands and smiled at her across the bar. "Though I can't promise what the town will think about me leaving your apartment mid-afternoon after a late night at the pub."

"Ah, shite," Fi swore and glanced out the window. The man was absolutely right, and wasn't that enough to put her in a mood?

CHAPTER 22

"What's this I hear Liam was seen leaving your place yesterday afternoon? And from Mary Margaret of all people, not even me own kin?" Gracie demanded when Fi strolled into the pub the next evening. She had come for a last pint with her family before her flight in the morning.

"And a good evening to you, Miss Gracie, it's lovely to see you've recuperated just fine from your hen party. Oh, and you're right welcome, you are, for me throwing you such a fine bash." Fi stuck a hand on her hip and narrowed her eyes at Grace.

"Oh, would you hush up? I was getting to all that, I was," Grace said. Then, jumping from the stool, she threw her arms around Fi, nearly bowling her over before dragging her to the bar. "It was the best hen party I've ever had."

"It's the only hen party you've ever had," Fi pointed out, settling onto a stool and smiling over at Cait, who was arguing with Mr. Murphy at the other end of the bar.

"Hello, Fi. Thank you for throwing my fiancée a lovely party the other night. She gushed about it all day long yesterday." Dylan leaned over from his seat next to Grace and smiled at her.

"There – *that's* a proper thank you. Unlike this ungrateful wench here," Fi sniffed.

"I swear to the goddess, if you don't give me the details on Liam, like, *now*, I'm going to throttle you." Gracie smacked her palm on the bar.

"Gracie, I'm sure you're not asking my own daughter if she slept with a man in front of her mum, are you?" Cait demanded from behind the bar.

Grace had the decency to blush. "No, ma'am, I'm not."

"That's a good girl. Now, Fi, you'd better be telling the truth about why Liam was seen leaving your apartment yesterday afternoon. No lying to your mum, now."

"Mum!" Fi blushed, "First off, you're the one who shoved me out onto the street with a drunken man. If anything did happen, you would be to blame."

"I most certainly did not shove you out on the street. I was making sure you didn't stay up all night cleaning. You'd think she'd appreciate her mum more," Cait sniffed, pouring out a glass of the red wine she knew Fi liked and passing it across the bar.

"I do appreciate you. Don't turn this around on me," Fi warned as she took a sip of the wine. "And Liam was at my place because he was too pissed to give me directions to his place. The man was asleep before he hit the bed, trust me on that."

"That's a good girl, then," Cait said, knowing without a

doubt when her daughter was telling the truth. "You're a good friend, Fi."

"I try to be," Fi said, and shot a look at Grace. "Even to the ungrateful ones."

"Oh, shut it. I'm grateful, I'm grateful. You're the best, best friend in all the world. But... what about..." Grace looked at Cait and then back to Fi.

"Liam? We're friends. That's all," Fi said, her tone final.

"Really? Gosh, I was kind of hoping for more."

"I understand that. But the timing is weird, things are a little complicated, and I like the man enough to want to keep him around as a mate."

"But what's complicated?" Grace asked, taking a sip of her whiskey.

"This." Fi pointed to Grace and then to Dylan, and then circled the air with her finger. "Too many overlapping friendships and business relationships. It's really just better this way, all in all."

"But what about..." Grace made sure Cait was on the other side of the pub. "You know."

"One night does not a relationship make, Gracie. So we have a wee history. It's nothing. We talked about it and we're fine to be friends. Truly."

"If you say so..." Grace didn't look convinced.

"Let her be, Grace. It sounds like they've figured it out just fine. No need to meddle in their business." Dylan wrapped an arm around Grace's waist and squeezed.

"Says the man who let Fi meddle in our future."

"That's because you were being bitchy and ignoring me."

"Excuse me?" Grace's attention turned, much to Fi's relief, and she relaxed as Grace battered Dylan with all the things he'd done to make her act bitchy at the time.

"What time is your flight again?" Cait asked, leaning over the bar.

"It's in the afternoon. Out of Shannon."

"And you'll be back when?"

"If all goes well, hopefully right before the wedding. At least according to Dylan."

"According to Dylan what?" Grace tuned back in.

"My next project. Dylan's hired me to review some contracts on a business merger."

"You did? You didn't tell me that. You're taking away my best friend right before my wedding?" Gracie pouted.

"You've plenty of help here," Dylan said, tugging on a strand of Gracie's curls, "and I can use her on this project."

"But…"

"But what? It should only be a few weeks," Dylan smiled.

"Fine, but if things get screwed up because Fi isn't here to micromanage everything, then you're in trouble," Grace warned.

"Duly noted," Dylan said and sipped his Guinness.

"And on that note, I have to go pack and finish up a few things at the house. Da is meeting me over there to show me how to shut down the electrics and whatnot." Fi pushed back from the bar, hugging both Grace and Dylan. "Don't fuss, Grace. I'll be back the week before and around to help with everything. I promise."

"Fine. Have fun in – where are you going?"

"Spain." Fi beamed.

"Fine. Enjoy your tapas and whatever. I'll be here. Slaving away."

"I'll be working, Gracie. It's a job. No more guilt tripping. Despite what you may think, the world does not stop and start because of your wedding."

"Oh, now she's being nasty," Grace said, pinching Fi's waist. "You'll regret that when I make you wear yellow for the wedding."

"You wouldn't," Fi said, stopping at the door in shock.

"I just might. I'll expect you back here one week before. Not a second later."

"Bridezilla," Fi called, waving to Cait on the way out. She'd see both her parents again before she left. Humming, she strolled down the sidewalk, her mind already on the trip and not what she was leaving behind.

WHEN LIAM WANDERED into the pub nearly fifteen minutes after Fi had left, Grace couldn't help but wonder at the timing of it all. Had they purposely planned to avoid each other? Grace's Cove was a small town; it was almost impossible to hide from someone.

"Hi Liam," Grace called, patting the stool Fi had just vacated. "Fancy a pint?"

"I'll have to pass. I'm just coming in to settle up my tab from the other night and say my goodbyes."

"Goodbyes?" Grace arched an eyebrow at Liam as Cait looked over her shoulder from where she rang up his bill at the till.

"Are you off on an adventure then, Liam?" Cait asked. Turning, she slid a piece of paper over to Liam.

"A small one. Dylan needs some help with a project he's overseeing in Spain."

"Does he now?" Grace said, turning to raise an eyebrow at Dylan.

Interpreting her mood as something related to the wedding, Liam grinned and patted her shoulder. "Don't worry, Grace. I should be back right before the wedding. If you need me to bring anything from abroad for the party, let me know. I'm happy to be a delivery boy for you."

"That's nice of you, Liam. I certainly appreciate it. I do love some of their wines. I'll get a list to you," Grace said, fluttering her lashes at him while she squeezed her hand tightly on Dylan's thigh.

"You do that. Dylan, I'll be in touch. Cait, as always, you run the best pub in all of Ireland."

"That I do. Don't you be forgetting that with those fancy Spaniards, now," Cait said, smiling at him as she cashed him out.

"I couldn't possibly. My heart belongs to your pub, I promise you that."

"Safe travels," Grace called sweetly. She waited until the door closed firmly behind Liam before swiveling to glare at Dylan.

"What?" Dylan asked, smiling at Grace.

"Don't meddle, the man says. Did you hear that, Cait?"

"I most certainly did hear that, Gracie."

"No meddling, he says. Don't be meddling in people's relationships, the man admonishes me!" Grace said, digging a finger into Dylan's waist.

"Ow!" Dylan laughed, grabbing her finger and bringing her hand to his lips. "I have no idea what you are talking about."

"You hired Fi for the Spain project."

"I did, at that."

"And it appears Liam is also heading to Spain."

"So it seems."

"Would it be for the same project then, Dylan?"

"Ah, yes, I'd have to check my records, but I do believe it might be the same project."

"You're a sneaky man, Dylan. It's what I like about you," Gracie decided. She turned when Cait bent below the bar, and watched her pull out a large leather-bound book.

Cait thumped the ledger on the bar and paged it open to a fresh sheet. "Okay, everyone – bets are open."

"Oh, I was waiting for this to happen!" Dylan exclaimed, digging in his pocket for his wallet. "It's my turn now."

"You've a wicked streak in you, love," Grace said, and turned to Cait. "I'll put fifty on three weeks from today."

CHAPTER 23

*H*er mother had been unduly chipper about her leaving for this trip, which raised Fi's suspicions enough that she almost – *almost* – dipped into Cait's thoughts. But it had been so long since she'd employed that particular part of herself that the ability felt rusty and unused. Deciding against it, Fi kept her well-honed shields in place and refrained from picking the thoughts from her mum's brain. But the fact that she'd even considered tapping into her power was odd, and she mulled the thought over as she waited in line for her flight at the airport.

Dylan had sprung for first class – which said a lot to Fi about the deal they were walking into – and she had two folders full of contracts to review on the flight to Barcelona. It was a welcome break from wedding planning and other personal things, Fi decided as she hitched the strap of her leather tote further up her shoulder and smiled at the flight attendant who took her passport.

"Enjoy your holiday." The flight attendant beamed at her.

"It's work. But I'm hoping to relax," Fi said and walked toward the plane, her mind already on the contracts and what she knew of Barcelona. She'd only been twice before, for no more than a week each time, and she'd really enjoyed the city. Hopefully there would be some downtime to explore and maybe get a little shopping in.

She loved flying, even more so when she had the opportunity to fly first class. Which wasn't that often, despite the caliber of the companies she worked for and what they paid her. Her mum's daughter to the core, Fi was more frugal than extravagant and really only spent her money when it was worth it. For example, she'd splurge on a nice leather tote that would last her for years and never go out of style, rather than buying three or four bags in the trendy colors of the season. A saver at heart, Fi had never splurged on first class for a plane ticket herself. She preferred upgrading to a nicer hotel room, or treating herself to a nice piece of art, rather than spending the money for a limited amount of time on a plane. However, when the company offered to cover her airfare, she had no problem indulging in certain luxuries. Smiling her hello at the first-class cabin attendant, Fi slipped into her seat and accepted a mimosa as a welcome drink. Relaxing, she sipped her drink and pulled out the first file folder Dylan had given her to familiarize herself with his merger. It was fascinating, really, to dip into his business and get an idea of the man Grace was marrying.

At first she hadn't been certain that a notorious

entrepreneur with a reputation across Europe would be a good fit for Grace, but after seeing them together, Fi could appreciate all the ways in which they balanced each other. Where Grace was fiery, Dylan tempered her with his calm and cool. Where Dylan could be ruthless, Grace offered him kindness. Together they were a great pair, and Fi looked forward to see where they would go together as partners.

"Well, this is a surprise."

Fi almost dropped her mimosa in her lap when she looked up to see Liam standing over her. Dressed for business in a grey suit coat and pressed slacks, he looked worlds away from the roughshod sailor who had woken up in her flat a few days ago.

"Liam! What are you doing here?" Fi asked, and for a moment her heart skipped a beat. Had he chased her down once he'd heard she was leaving?

"It appears I'm going to Barcelona, as are you. I didn't know this was your next project," Liam said, checking his ticket and settling into the seat next to her.

"I didn't know you were on another project at all," Fi said, lifting her chin at him. She waited while the flight attendant asked him his drink choice. Sipping her mimosa, she let the pieces fall into place. They had both worked for Dylan at different points in their careers. It wasn't coincidence that they were headed to the same project at the same time.

"Dylan asked me yesterday to fly down and see to a few things. I take it he did the same for you?"

"Yes, he asked me a few days ago if I'd take over translations for the merger."

"Ah," Liam said, nodding his thanks to the attendant when she placed a beer in front of him. "I suppose I can see what he's up to."

"Meddling," Fi sniffed.

"He might be at that, but I've never known Dylan to let personal interfere with business. He wouldn't hire you for the job if he didn't think you were qualified. Even if he does want me to get laid."

Fi choked on the sip she'd just taken, and despite herself, she threw her head back and laughed.

"Okay, that's fair enough. You're right. I am qualified to handle this merger, and I presume you're qualified to do whatever it is you're doing on this, so, I suppose... cheers, partner," Fi said, offering her cup to him.

"Slainté," Liam said, touching his cup to hers, before taking a long drink.

"What can you tell me about the project?" Fi asked, deciding it was best to switch into work mode. It wouldn't do for her head to go down the road of Liam's 'getting laid' comment. No, that wouldn't do at all.

"He's been wanting to switch to a different shipping company for one of his rental car companies. We export many of our cars from Spain and haven't been happy with the costs or the environmental practices of the cargo ship. This new company seems to be not only more expedient, but much more environmentally friendly in their practices."

"Rental cars? I didn't know Dylan was in that market."

"Electric cars, actually. He's working on building a better fleet of rental cars for tourists who care more about the environment. It's been quite profitable, and I think it makes him happy. I'm not too sure about this company we're merging with – my research into them seems to keep hitting dead ends. Which is another reason I'm going to oversee the merger. If I feel like anything is off, we'll pull out."

"Wow, Dylan trusts you that much?" Fi asked, then winced at the wounded look on Liam's face.

"Despite how I may look, I'm a fairly competent business analyst."

"I'm sorry, that was rude of me. I know you're competent. I just meant he must trust you a lot if you have the ability to pull the plug on a..." Fi flipped through her folder, then finished, "Ten-million-euro contract."

"Yes. I've earned his trust," Liam said.

Fi sighed and flipped the folder closed. Reaching out, she squeezed Liam's arm.

"Truly, I didn't mean to be sounding callous with you. I'm just not used to making deals at that level, so I imagined there would be more people involved in making the decision to call off something at that level is all."

"My feelings are hurt." Liam sniffed and looked away.

Fi smiled, because she knew he was playing at this point. "What can I do to make it up to you?"

"Have dinner with me."

"That sounds like a date," Fi cautioned.

"It sounds like two friends lonely in a big city together needing sustenance."

"So long as it remains as that," Fi sighed, and finished off her drink as the attendants went around the plane readying them for take-off.

"We'll take it a dinner at a time," Liam decided.

Fi rolled her eyes, biting back a laugh as the captain called for takeoff and they prepared to leave the green hills of Ireland behind them.

CHAPTER 24

"I assume Dylan has booked us at the same hotel then?" Fi asked as they walked to the taxi stand at the airport.

The flight had been relatively uneventful, except for when Fi had tried to pass off their in-flight meal as the dinner she had agreed to have with Liam. Fi laughed when he threatened to force her to be his tour guide for the entire three weeks instead of joining him for a dinner, then quickly acquiesced and kept to their original arrangement.

"He has me booked at a hotel called the One," Liam said, sliding a glance her way and then toward the line of taxis waiting outside.

Fi decided not to comment on the hotel name, though she wondered if there was subliminal messaging there. Not exactly subtle, her friend's fiancé, was he?

"Is that really the name?"

"It actually is. I've stayed there before," Liam said with a laugh, and held the door of the taxi for her.

Fi smiled and addressed the taxi driver in fluent Spanish. "*Hola, nos quedaremos en el hotel llamado* the One *en el centro de la ciudad.*"

Liam glanced at her and smiled.

"What?" Fi asked.

"I like hearing you speak Spanish. It's sexy."

"Thanks. Friend," Fi said, putting extra emphasis on the word. Turning, she looked out the window as the taxi wound its way toward the city center. She liked the architecture of Barcelona, where some streets were cobblestoned, houses and flats clustered on top of each other, and winding alleyways led to delightful little restaurants. It was a city she could wander in, and she hoped to find time to get lost for a while at some point during the trip. It was something she often enjoyed doing when she had a free afternoon. She would wander a city at her whim, turning when she felt like it and seeing where she ended up.

Liam was likely a wanderer as well, Fi thought as she studied his face. This Liam was a different Liam than the one she knew – the one who checked his watch and the neat little smartphone in his palm, making sure the time synchronized on both. She'd be lying to herself if she said Liam in a business suit was any less handsome than Liam in his dock clothes. Maybe it was just Liam, Fi thought, and turned her head to look out at the city once more. The man was handsome in anything he wore… and even more so without clothes.

Heat rose to Fi's face at the thought. Hoping he didn't notice it, she jumped into a conversation with the taxi driver about the best restaurants surrounding their hotel.

Satisfied with his answers, Fi smiled as they pulled up to an impressive hotel, all sleek lines and shiny windows.

It would be perfect for business, but not something Fi would have chosen on her own. She preferred small in-the-corner type places – the bed-and-breakfasts and locally-owned spots. It was there she would get the best tips for restaurants or outings, because the people who ran them cared about their guests and made extra time for them.

After going through the check-in routine, they made their way to the elevator tucked across from reception. The foyer was sleek and modern, done up in whites and blues with touches of gold. At least it wasn't fussy, Fi thought as she stopped to wait for the elevator.

"What floor are you?" Liam asked as the doors opened.

"Why do you need to know?" Fi parried.

"So I can press the button?" Liam quirked an eyebrow at her and Fi rolled her eyes, reaching over to push the button for the eleventh floor. When Liam didn't push a different button, she sighed.

"Same floor?"

"Correct. Imagine that," Liam grinned, rocking back on his heels. "I'm sure Dylan's arranged that for convenience. We'll likely be having just about the same schedule each day."

"I'm sure," Fi murmured, striding out of the elevator and into a long hallway in subdued greys with gentle lighting. "Have a good night then."

"Wait, I thought we had dinner," Liam said from behind her.

Fi turned. "Tonight?"

"Sure, why not?"

"Because I wanted to read over those contracts."

"You read them on the plane. I watched you."

"Maybe I want to read them again."

"It's barely four in the afternoon. And everybody eats late in Spain. Say nine for dinner?"

"Is this the dinner I owe you?"

"Sure." Liam smiled at her and warmth flooded her core.

"Fine. I'll see you in the lobby at nine."

"I'll meet you at your door," Liam countered. "What should I wear?"

"Why are you asking me?"

"It's your dinner. You pick the restaurant."

"Jeans and a nice shirt should be fine. We're going casual."

"Perfect by me. I'm sure you'll have a great spot to wow me with."

"I'm just going off the taxi driver's recommendation. It could be a food truck for all you know."

"I've had some of my best meals at food trucks."

"Damn it," Fi laughed, and slid her key into the slot in the door, "so have I."

"See you later," Liam called.

Fi let the door click closed behind her. The room was lovely, though not very large, as to be expected with European hotels. But the bed looked comfortable, there was a lovely workstation for her by the window, and she had the added bonus of a lounge chair to relax in. After she freshened up in the bathroom, Fi dropped into the chair and slid the curtains open to look out over Barcelona. Below her, the city bustled with life, and Fi took a deep breath, happy to be back in the mix of work and city life.

Checking her schedule, she emailed a confirmation for

her meeting with Luis Dominado, the CEO of the shipping company hoping to contract with Dylan's company, which was to happen at eleven the next morning. The most important part of her job was to make sure that any contracts Dylan ended up signing reflected not only the exact language, but also the exact interpretation – under any applicable laws – in both languages. In international deals, it could be tricky if contracts were signed that left the interpretations open or were not precisely translated. Her job was to make sure that everything was as clear as it could be for all parties involved.

Pushing everything aside, Fi lost herself in her work, and several hours passed before she looked up at the clock.

"Shite," Fi said, realizing that she would need some time to shower and get ready. Pushing the papers aside, she dashed to her suitcase to unpack. Pulling out a simple black dress, she studied it for a moment and then put it aside. "Just friends, Fi."

The knock sounded on her door precisely at nine; Fi had to give the man credit for being prompt. Breathing out a sigh, she studied herself in the floor-length mirror by the door. A deep red shirt that twisted in a knot at her waist was paired with skinny jeans and gold sandals. She'd hung large gold hoops at her ears and dusted some tawny makeup across her eyes. All in all, she thought she looked nice, but not like she was trying too hard. Though why she even cared... Fi shook her head and grabbed her purse.

"Wow, you look amazing," Liam immediately commented, and Fi had to admit – so did he. In a pair of dark jeans and a fitted linen shirt with the sleeves rolled to his elbows, he looked comfortable, confident, and every inch a man.

"Thank you. You do as well. Though why it matters for a friendly dinner, I do not know," Fi said, sticking her nose in the air a bit.

"Friends can give each other compliments," Liam reminded her as they walked to the elevator.

"You're absolutely right. I have no idea why I'm being a bitch. Must be that time of the month." Fi smiled and then let out a laugh when Liam winced.

"Um…"

"What? Friends talk about that stuff. Right, buddy?"

Fi laughed the whole way to the lobby.

CHAPTER 25

They went for tapas, as one does in Spain, and Fi was pleased she'd listened to the taxi driver's recommendation. Instead of a fancy restaurant, they wandered down a curving alley that led them to a small restaurant with an arched doorway. The proprietor looked up, beaming his welcome, his smile widening when Fi greeted him in Spanish. Chattering away, he led them to the back, away from the bar where people could stand and eat their tapas, to a table tucked under a curved brick alcove.

"I'm assuming you'll be fine with staying in one spot? Or did you want to move to different restaurants for your tapas tonight?" Fi asked Liam, smiling as the owner handed her a small sheet of paper with the wine list and the day's menu on it.

"I'm fine with settling in here. It's been a long few days and I'm more than happy to be relaxing in one spot with a lovely lass on my arm." Liam grinned at her, and Fi almost fired back at him before she caught the twinkle in his eye.

"This lovely lass is starving," Fi said and looked at him over the sheet of paper in her hand. "Mind if I order for us?"

"Be my guest." Liam waved a hand at her and Fi turned to converse with the owner. They discussed several of the wines and picked some lovely dishes. As they chatted, Fi learned he'd started in the restaurant as a cook and had worked his way up to owning it through the years. Now his boy cooked in the kitchen and his wife ran the bar. Fi told him who had recommended the restaurant to her and promised to visit again before their stay was over. Pleased with her comments, the owner beamed and clapped his hands, shouting to his wife in rapid Spanish. The wife, a gently rounded woman with shining brown eyes and hair that curled softly around her shoulders, appeared at his side with a bottle of wine. Together, they made a big flourish of popping the cork and waiting for Fi's approval before pouring them each a glass. Leaving the bottle, the owner smiled to them both before moving to greet new guests who had entered the restaurant.

"He seems nice. Cheerful," Liam commented.

"He is. The woman is his wife; he used to be a line chef before working his way all the way up to being the owner. I like places like this, because they'll be proud of their food. It might not always be the fanciest, but I suspect each dish will be made with love and the ingredients sourced with care."

"I love watching you when you talk to someone in a different language. Is that what drew you into doing translations?" Liam held his glass up, lightly touching the rim to hers, the light making the wine look molten in the glass.

"Yes, partially, I suppose." Fi leaned back and smiled her thanks when the first course, a plate of cut meat with a dish of olives, was brought to the table. She took a sip of her wine. Delicious, as expected – she so loved Spanish wines. "I view language as a bridge. We're lucky to speak English, as it is a fairly common language around the world and you can often get by in other countries with it. But I love seeing people's face light up when they know I can meet them on their level and communicate with them. It opens things up for me, and I've been able to learn more about the world because of that. For example, I doubt we would have found this restaurant if I hadn't been able to speak to the taxi driver. Or a million other little tips I've been given through the years, or experiences I've been able to have because I can navigate my way through a different language."

"You love it then... the travel and the new experiences? You don't want to settle down?" Liam asked, sampling a marinated olive.

"I don't know that I crave settling down in the same way most people do, I'll be admitting that." Fi pursed her lips and studied the plate of food before picking out a slice of meat.

"How do you see most people wanting to settle down?"

"Oh, well you know how it is – married, babies, house, a dog... those things."

"Do you view that as settling?"

"I... well, hmm... I guess I've never put much thought

into it, have I, now?" Fi chewed for a moment, enjoying the spicy flavors, and took a sip from her glass. The wine perfectly highlighted the meat, and she looked forward to the rest of their dishes. "I shouldn't say that I think people who choose that path are settling, because that makes it sound like that way of life isn't good enough. Or is less than what it could be. And that's really not a fair thing to be thinking, especially as some of me own family are deeply happy with those choices. So, what I mean to be saying is that I don't think people who choose that are settling as in accepting less than they should out of life. But I do mean settle in the actual literal sense. As in settled into a home and they'll be staying put for a while."

Liam grinned at her across the table and Fi glared at him.

"Sure and I know I'm rambling a bit, but I'm just teasing out the thought."

"I understand what you're saying. You feel as though that particular lifestyle might feel confining to you."

"There! That's a lovely way of putting it. Gracie and I always go back and forth on this. She's as content as can be up in her cottage on the cliffs. Never wants for more and loves her life. Me? I'd be going mental, sure as the day is long. I get… restless, I suppose? I crave new adventures. I love traveling and seeing what's over the next horizon."

"I can be understanding that. I've sailor's blood in me, after all." Liam grinned at her once more and Fi found herself smiling back at him. No matter what lay between them, she genuinely enjoyed Liam's company.

"What took you to the water then?"

"Me own da was a fisherman. Right out of Kinsale. I

grew up more comfortable on the water than on land. He worked for Flynn, did ye know?"

"Did he now? I didn't know that. My, we do have many overlapping connections, don't we?" Fi said.

She looked up when the owner arrived with the next course. This one was a lovely browned tortilla de patatas and Fi's eyes lit up at the presentation. Making approving comments and noises over the dish, Fi turned her attention back to Liam once the owner had been roundly assured he had the best tortilla de patatas in all the land.

"So it seems," Liam said, picking up the thread of their conversation.

"However, I wasn't ever keen to be a commercial fisherman meself, so I took to university to see what else I could learn."

"Which is where you met Dylan?"

"I met him after university. I got him out of a bit of trouble at a pub in Dubs and we formed a fast friendship after that. Turns out, our interests ran parallel."

"A bit of trouble? And what would that have been about?"

Liam only smiled at her across the table before taking a bite of the tortilla. "This is delicious," he said.

Fi rolled her eyes. "Fine, you'll protect your mates to the end. I get it. So, you hooked up with Dylan and he just hired you like that?"

"Not too long after that. I've been working with him ever since. I was particularly pleased with some of his sailing charters and happy to be on the voyages. He was particularly pleased with my attention to detail and ability to manage others well. He trusts me, and I him."

"Sometimes working together can be a strain on a relationship. Have you found that to be true?"

"Not thus far. So long as we're being honest with each other. Honesty is never frowned upon in business, and Dylan and I are straight with each other. I may not always like what he has to say," Liam said, and shrugged his wide shoulders, "but I appreciate an honest voice rather than one that is only looking out for his business."

"He doesn't just put money first?"

"Don't get me wrong, the man likes to make money. And he's damn good at it, lucky for me. But it isn't his bottom line."

"How can it not be his bottom line? Doesn't he want his business to be profitable?"

"His businesses can be profitable and ethical at the same time. There's no contradiction there, me lovely lass," Liam said, trying it out again. He chuckled when Fi bared her teeth at him across the table.

"It's nice to hear good things about Dylan from someone besides Grace. From what I've Googled of him he seems to have a good reputation in business. But it's also nice to be hearing it from someone close to him as well."

"And Gracie? She's magick, no? Is that comfortable for you?"

Fi opened her mouth and then closed it, shocked at his question. Nobody outside their circle had ever outright asked her a question like that, and now she found herself struggling with how to respond.

Taking a moment, she picked up the wine bottle and poured them each another glass before looking out across the restaurant, which was now filling up. She had no idea how much Grace had told Dylan or Liam about her magick, though she knew that Grace had healed Liam after his mishap in the cove.

"She's a healer, yes," Fi said, looking down at the tortilla and carefully cutting herself another bite. Putting the bite in her mouth, she savored the flavors and hoped Liam would move on.

"So, you get to be grilling me on Dylan, but I'm not able to ask after Gracie?" Liam raised an eyebrow at Fi before taking a long sip of his wine. Over the speakers, a light dancy violin solo came on, threading its notes through the chatter of the people in the restaurant.

"No, you can ask after her," Fi said, looking away from Liam again as she considered her answer. She'd never had to speak with anyone about this and wasn't entirely sure what was best.

"I've made you uncomfortable," Liam observed, leaning back in his chair to study her.

Fi met his eyes and then looked away again. "I'm comfortable."

"And now she's a liar?"

"What makes you think I'm uncomfortable?" Fi parried.

"I'm good at reading people. I study body language, facial expressions, and so on. Your energy went from bright and open to being totally closed off."

"She's my best friend," Fi said, taking another sip of her wine.

"As Dylan is mine. I mean no disrespect to Grace. I owe her my life." Liam reached across the table and ran a finger across the back of Fi's hand, drawing her gaze to their hands and then up to his eyes. "I would never do anything to hurt her; I'm forever indebted to her. I would protect her with my life, as I would her secrets. You must be understanding that at the very least."

Fi blew out a breath and pulled her hand away from Liam's. The closeness was making her feel all sorts of things, and the color of his aura was beginning to show around his shoulders. A nice healthy blue, she noted. Blue auras represented truthfulness to her. She typically found people with those auras to be leaders, creatives, and generally all-around solid people. Not to mention it matched the sea, Fi thought, then pulled herself away from thinking about his aura. It wasn't something she liked to dwell on very often, but she'd be lying to herself if she didn't trust what an aura showed her. "I guess it's because I've never had a conversation with someone outside the circle about it."

"There's a circle, is there?" Liam asked, leaning back as the proprietor came and cleaned plates, putting down a selection of fruits and cheeses for their next round. Fi chattered with him, hoping Liam would forget his question, but knowing instinctively he would not.

"I just meant like our close circle of friends. Obviously Grace's friends and family are aware of her talents."

"I think it's incredible. Doesn't it just wow you?" Liam's eyes lit up with excitement. "It's the reason sailors look for mermaids and read old mythological lore. We go our whole lives hoping for a glimpse of something like this. To experience it firsthand? It was a true blessing, that it was. Like an angel herself, Gracie is."

"It's tough to say where the energy comes from," Fi agreed, careful with her words, "but I definitely believe there's a spiritual element there."

"Are you Catholic?"

Letting out a small breath, happy for the change of subject, Fi shrugged a shoulder. "Not really. It wasn't something strongly reinforced in our home. Mum felt like we could make our own decisions about religion as we grew older. I never really took to it myself."

"I'm not a fan of organized religion either. I think nature is religion enough, no?" Liam smiled at her and Fi found herself smiling back, drinking in his eyes.

"A pagan, then, are you?"

"I suppose I'd be something along that line. I believe in Mother Ocean and the rhythms of nature more than anything. Nature always finds a way."

"That it does," Fi agreed. "Do you have much of a family, Liam?"

"Sure and you don't think I was a foundling, do you?" Liam chuckled and leaned back in his chair once more to study her. "I do at that. I've told you of my father, the fisherman. Mum was a schoolteacher, and a strict one. She had to be, with five boys underfoot."

"Five!" Fi almost choked on her sip of wine. "The poor woman."

"Aye, and she's letting us know that every day of our lives. A good woman, she is. Kept us in line. My brothers and I are close, though we're scattered about the globe."

"That's nice. I always dreamed about having a brother or sister. Gracie was the closest to me like that. And Kira, though she was a bit younger."

"Your parents didn't want more?"

"No, my mum was a bit of a reluctant mother, though she loves fiercely. I couldn't have asked for a better mum than her. But she was content with just one child. The pub's her other."

"It's a fine pub."

"It really is," Fi agreed. "I was raised at the helm. If you're ever wanting to open a business like that, she's the woman to give you tips."

"I've thought about it, a time or two. But I like being able to get up and go when I like. You can't do that with a pub that needs opening every day."

"You can if you hire the right manager."

"'Tis true, 'tis true. Maybe someday when I'm not set on wandering. Speaking of wandering, shall we head back to the hotel?"

"What time is it?"

"It's already eleven thirty." Liam smiled at her shock and waved to the owner. "I imagine you'll want a clear head for the morning."

"I will." Fi leaned over and squeezed Liam's hand, content with their meal and their conversation. "This was nice. I'm glad we did this and that you're here. It's nice to have a friend on your travels."

"To friends," Liam said, and they both finished off their wine. Fi ignored the little tug of lust that played through her core, as well as the voice in her head that begged her for more from Liam. At this point, he was a business partner and needed to remain such.

CHAPTER 26

She slept straight through to morning in her deliciously comfortable hotel bed, having for once been afforded a dreamless sleep. Perhaps it was the wine that had slipped her into oblivion, and if so, Fi wasn't complaining. It was nice not to wake up in a riot of turmoil or unease, and she enjoyed an espresso in her room while she read through the papers she'd had delivered up. Her mood was good this morning, she'd enjoyed a nice dinner, this job should be an interesting one, and she had a few weeks to explore Barcelona. All in all, not a bad start to the week.

Pairing trim black pants with a black blazer and a muted rose blouse, Fi smoothed her hair back and clipped a delicate silver necklace around her neck. Slipping her feet into low-heeled boots, she doublechecked her tote to make sure she had all her supplies – laptop, notebook, contracts, and pens. Satisfied, she took the elevator to the lobby, smiling at the concierge as she crossed the gleaming floor to wait for a taxi. Her meeting was at the shipyard, so she'd get an opportunity to also look over the boats and see how the operation worked. Not that it mattered much, as that was Liam's department, but it always interested her to see how different businesses were run.

"Going my way?"

Fi turned and smiled at Liam as he crossed to her side. The man wore a suit well, she decided as she took in his dusty grey suit and crisp white shirt. He was the kind of man who wore his clothes casually, as though to say he'd rather be in jeans, and his lack of care in how he carried himself only added to his confident air.

"Will you be attending the meeting at the shipyard at eleven?" Fi asked.

"I will. Would it be presumptuous of me to comment on how you look today? Seeing as we're in business mode?" Liam's lips quirked a small smile.

"It would be at that." Fi pressed a smile back and slid into the taxi, waiting as Liam rounded the car and sat next to her.

"Then I shall refrain from telling you that you look delectable in that suit. It makes me want to unbutton you and see what lies beneath all the prim and proper."

Heat flashed through Fi and she was certain her cheeks tinted pink. Grateful for the wide sunglasses she'd pulled on, she turned and leveled a look at Liam.

"That was rude of me, wasn't it?" Liam held up his hands, though his smile said he didn't care.

"You shouldn't be harassing a colleague," Fi pointed out.

Instantly contrite, Liam put his hands down.

"You're right. I'm sorry, I was having a wee bit of fun

of with you. I suppose I feel like I can overstep my boundaries with you, and I really shouldn't. My apologies.
During work hours, I'll treat you with the utmost respect."

"And after work hours?"

"Depends on if you've asked me to disrespect you or
not." Liam's voice held a low timbre that sent lust roiling
through Fi once again.

"I'll remember that," Fi said and turned to watch the
city go by. They lapsed into a comfortable silence, and Fi
was grateful for a moment to work on her composure. She
had to admire Liam. Every time he overstepped a
boundary with her and she called him on it, he respected
her wishes and eased off. It was a delicate dance of him
testing where her limits were and her showing him. She
respected him for trying, but also for backing off when
asked. Last night, when they'd wound their way back to
the hotel – they'd opted to walk back – she'd been certain
he would try to hold her hand or make a move on her at the
door to her hotel room. Instead, he'd been ever the gentleman, walking companionably by her side and seeing her to
her door with zero pressure for anything more. Not even a
goodnight kiss, which she'd been certain he would try for.
It left her feeling oddly bereft, a part of her wanting more.
But as she'd set the rules, it was on her to abide by them as
well.

It also left her wondering what was wrong with her that
she wouldn't be interested in dating a great guy like Liam.
She'd dated far worse in her past, and it was beginning to
get a bit blurry in her mind about just why she'd decided
they needed to only be friends. Away from the watchful

eyes of family and friends, a relationship with Liam didn't seem so complicated anymore.

The taxi pulled to a stop at two large metal gates to the shipyard. Glancing over his shoulder, the driver looked at her in question.

"*Sí, bien.*"

A man exited a door by the gate and strode toward them, a smile on his face. Tanned, wearing mirrored glasses that shaded his eyes and a slim-cut suit in navy, he looked every inch the successful Spanish businessman. Despite having just had thoughts about Liam, Fi found herself admiring this man. He was the type she usually went for – polished, well-to-do businessmen. When Liam rounded the boot of the taxi and held out his hand, Fi had to stop herself from letting out a little sigh. Both handsome in their own right – one refined and wiry, the other broad and a bit rough and tumble – she'd be hard-pressed to say which she preferred.

"And you must be Fiona." The man turned and gave her a blinding smile, holding out his hands. "I'm Luis. I'll be working with you on this project."

"Ah, thank you, Luis. It's nice to meet you," Fi said, turning to follow him onto the grounds.

"And here is our shipyard. My English, it is not so good. Do you mind?" With that, Luis launched into Spanish, effectively cutting Liam out, and Fi followed him, carrying on the conversation. For the most part, he chatted about the ships as he led them across a gravel courtyard to a long grey cinderblock building. Luis chattered on, pointing out the various attributes of the vessels, while Fi did her best to translate quickly for Liam. When they went inside, Luis began to ask Fi about her life and family.

"Do you travel much for work?"

"I do, yes. I quite enjoy it."

"Your husband doesn't mind?"

"No husband." Fi smiled.

"A beautiful woman such as yourself? I'm shocked," Luis said, removing his glasses to reveal liquid brown eyes.

"We all make choices, Luis," Fi said, putting a little sass into her words. She wanted to push back at him just a bit.

"I suppose. Work can cause one to sacrifice in other areas. Please, if you are here alone, allow me to treat you to dinner this evening. On the business, of course." Luis smiled and Fi warmed to him. "I know what it is to be alone in a different city."

"That would be nice, thank you."

"Lovely. I will collect you at your hotel at nine. Which hotel?"

"The One."

"Perfect. Now, shall we get to business?" Luis pushed open a glass door to a conference room. Windows lined one wall, and the view of the shipyard and the water beyond it was unobscured. On the table sat stacks of documents and an array of notebooks. A sideboard was stocked with coffee and an arrangement of pastries.

"Coffee?"

"Please. Liam? Coffee?"

"Tea for me," Liam said, and Fi couldn't help but notice Luis sniff at his choice.

"Of course."

"Hot date tonight?" Liam whispered to Fi.

"Why would you think that?"

"I know when a man is asking a woman out."

"He didn't want me to dine alone here. He said it's on the business." Fi shrugged.

"If so, why hasn't he asked me to dinner? Or tried to include me in the conversation?"

"Maybe he thinks you're annoying," Fi teased and smiled at Luis when he returned with a coffee for her. He'd left the tea on the sideboard, forcing Liam to go pick up the cup. Liam turned and raised an eyebrow at Fi, but she just shook her head slightly.

"Shall we begin?" Fi asked, and Luis nodded, looking from her to Liam.

"You'll provide translation for our discussions, then?"

"Of course," Fi said, and they bent to work, pushing everything else aside so they could hammer out the details of the contract. Watching Liam work was fascinating, Fi realized, for he truly knew the ins and outs of mergers like this one, and all of his questions were razor-sharp. As the hours drew on, her admiration for both men grew.

"Ah, I believe that is enough for one day." Luis looked pained, glancing at his watch. "I do have a lunch appointment."

Fi looked at her tablet. It was three o'clock, and she was once again reminded of the eating schedule of the Spanish. She'd have to recalibrate while she was here.

"I'd like a look around the boatyard, if you don't mind?"

"I'm afraid that is not possible without an escort.

Tomorrow, for sure," Luis said, and neatly handed them off with nothing more than a polite nod for Fi.

"I don't like him," Liam decided as they waited for a taxi.

Fi looked at him in shock. "What? Why?"

"I just don't. I don't like his vibe. He shouldn't be asking you to dinner."

"You're jealous," Fi laughed, astonished at his comments.

"I'm not jealous. I'm telling you I don't like him."

"I think you're letting personal cloud your business thoughts."

"Maybe I am. But if it was just business – why didn't he ask me to dinner?"

"As I said. Maybe he just thinks you're annoying? Like I do?" Fi shot him a look over her shoulder before sliding into the taxi.

"Doubtful. You think I'm charming, but won't let yourself think too much about it. However, the polite thing would have been for Luis to invite us both so we can all get to know each other better."

"Don't worry, Liam. Maybe he'll take you to dinner tomorrow." Fi laughed again, then sighed when he just shook his head and looked out the window.

And this was why she didn't want to be in a relationship, Fi reminded herself.

CHAPTER 27

Fi chose a simple black shift dress with a tailored matching cardigan to wear for dinner that evening. Opting for just a swipe of lip gloss, delicate diamond studs, and no eye makeup, she felt like she conveyed an appropriate appearance for a work dinner. Not that she should be judged on her outfit to convey any sort of meaning, but as a woman in the business world she often viewed her clothing as a suit of armor. Some days she wanted to look like she was going into battle, while on others she preferred a softer approach. Either way, despite the advancement of women in the business world, they were still judged on their appearance.

"You did judge Luis and Liam in their suits today," Fi said out loud to herself as she grabbed a quilted black Chanel purse to go with her dress. If she was being fair, maybe everyone just judged everyone else on their appearances – men or women. Either way, she felt she looked professional for her dinner, and looked forward to an insider's choice of restaurants in Barcelona. Humming softly to herself, she took the elevator down to the lobby and strode outside – to find Luis leaning against a black town car.

"Ah, you're early," Fi said, quickly checking the slim watch at her wrist. "My apologies for making you wait."

"I'll always wait for a beautiful woman," Luis said, bending to place a kiss on each of her cheeks. Fi's back went up; she hoped this dinner wouldn't result in her having to fend off unwanted advances. Catching a whiff of a soapy aftershave, Fi was happy he hadn't doused himself in cologne. She couldn't stand when people applied too much perfume or aftershave; it made her eyes water and brought on a headache.

Sliding onto the leather seat across from her, Luis ordered the driver to leave. "How was the rest of your day? Have you had a chance to enjoy our fair city?" Luis asked, turning to her. Clasping her hands in her lap, Fi angled her body slightly away from him, keeping her body language professional, and smiled at Luis in the dim light of the car.

"I had a lovely lunch by the water and was able to catch up on a book I've been meaning to finish for a while now."

"What are you reading?"

"Ah, you'll laugh," Fi said, blushing a bit.

"Try me."

"Well," Fi said, looking around the car guiltily, "it was actually one of the Harry Potter books. I've heard such great things, but always thought they were just for children until someone convinced me to give them a try."

"Harry Potter?" Luis slapped his leg and laughed. "They are my favorite!"

"Really?" Fi laughed, delighted with his reaction. She

had wondered if he would be a stuffy businessman who wouldn't lower himself to read such books. "I'm finding them quite an enjoyable escape."

"They're great. Why shouldn't they be? They're lovely entertainment with a world of magic. It's fun to imagine, no?"

"I agree, it is." Fi offered Luis a warm smile and he responded in kind.

The restaurant was sleek – way fancier than the one the night before – and she could tell that Luis was a regular here by the way the maître d' addressed him by name. Everything was flashy – from the Lucite chairs at the dinner tables that made Fi feel like she might fall to the floor when she sat down to the shiny gold wine glasses. Chandeliers dripped crystals from the ceiling, and the people of the room matched its glitz. Fi felt woefully underdressed in her simple dress and cardigan; the other women here were shiny, unapologetically sexy, and dripping in gems.

"Quite a place," Fi murmured, wishing for a moment to be back in the restaurant she'd visited with Liam the night before. It was more her speed. That being said, any locally-owned corner restaurant or pub would always be her comfort zone – it was what she'd been raised in. Traveling was meant to put her out of her comfort zone, so even if she didn't have the glitz of the rest of the people at the restaurant, she certainly had the smarts and the world experience.

"Do you like it? I wasn't sure if you'd go for fancy or not," Luis said.

"Not always, but here and there it's fun," Fi said,

reminding herself that this was a man who loved Harry Potter.

"Would you like to look at the menu or shall I order for both of us?"

"You obviously come here often. I'm adventurous with food, so you're welcome to order for me," Fi said. She leaned back in her chair to watch as Luis spoke with the waiter in detail about the specials for the evening. Shifting in her chair, she wondered why anyone would choose Lucite for a seat – it felt awkward and uncomfortable to her. Maybe that was why so many people were up and navigating around the restaurant. Though to her it looked like many of them knew each other. Perhaps this was just the evening hang-out for the wealthy of Barcelona.

"Now, tell me. You're Irish, no?"

"I am."

"How did you…?" Luis paused, nodding at the waiter who proffered a bottle of wine. They went through the sniff-and-taste dance, Luis swirling the liquid in the glass while Fi waited patiently for the routine to be over.

"Salud," Luis said.

"Sláinte," Fi said, reverting to her Irish.

"So… why being a translator?" Luis asked.

"I've always loved to travel. And I find that learning a language bridges a gap – it helps you into different countries and cultures in a way that you can't get if you don't speak their language."

"Ah, yes. Very smart. I also love to travel. It's why I love being in the shipping business. New horizons. Places to visit, explore." Luis waved a hand.

"Do you have a favorite spot to travel?"

"I adore the Swiss Alps. Do you ski?"

"Not very well, no."

"And Cannes is nice if you enjoy the festival."

Fi took a moment to sort that comment out.

"Do you mean the actual Cannes Film Festival? No, I can't say I've been."

"You haven't?" His handsome face registered surprise. Apparently, in his world, the Cannes Film Festival was a given.

"No, I've been quite busy during that time." Fi almost rolled her eyes but didn't.

"You'll have to go sometime. Or Monte Carlo?" Luis looked at her hopefully.

"I've been to Monte Carlo." Fi didn't say that she had left the same day, for the same reasons she wasn't a huge fan of this restaurant. Too much excess for her.

"Ah, yes. Did you gamble?"

"I'm afraid I did not. Work, you know," Fi said and turned as the waiter brought their first dish.

"Ahh, a lovely salad. Thank you, Miguel," Luis smiled. "So, you are very busy then. With work?"

"Yes and no. I will have down time between projects. I typically use that time to visit family or friends. Or if I particularly like the country I'm in, I'll take a few weeks to explore."

"On your own?" Luis asked, nodding at her in approval. "Not many people can do that. I admire that trait."

"I don't mind exploring alone. There's so much to learn in each city. There are museums, music, local craft fairs…" Fi smiled at Luis' look of horror. "You don't seem like the type to go to a craft fair."

"I'll admit, I do have a taste for… fancier items." Luis managed a look of chagrin. "I fear that may make me a bit of a snob."

"It's not so bad if you admit it." Fi laughed at the relieved look that passed over Luis' face.

"Tell me. These craft fairs. What do you find?"

"Oh, things like hand-beaded jewelry, intricately woven scarves, some lovely artwork… that kind of stuff. You'd be surprised at the undiscovered talent you can find there."

"Hmm, maybe one day I'll try one out." Luis smiled.

"I think I would like to see that, simply to see you out of your comfort zone," Fi decided, and laughed at the look that crossed Luis' face. "You don't strike me as someone who likes being uncomfortable."

"Generally, I shall admit, I do not. But that is not how you learn, no? It is best to try new things and then you grow."

"I agree. Which is why I love travel so much." Now that he had admitted his taste for opulence, Fi felt much more comfortable with him. The rest of the evening passed in a surprisingly easy manner, and Fi was glad she'd agreed to dinner. If anything, by the end of the night she'd warmed up to his charm and had been able to take him down a peg or two to make him more relatable.

When the town car pulled up at the hotel, Fi turned to thank him for dinner. "Dinner was lovely, Luis. Thank you for sharing part of your great city with me."

"Thank you for dining with me. I trust you'll enjoy

your time in Barcelona while you're here. Perhaps we can do this again. We can invite Liam along as well, if he would like to join us?"

Ha! Fi thought. Liam had Luis pegged wrong.

"I suspect he'd love to be included. Thank you for the offer."

"Rest well this evening. I will see you tomorrow," Luis said, exiting the car and holding the door open for her. Fi was pleased, and relieved, when he did nothing more than kiss her cheeks twice as a goodbye, which she knew was common as both a hello and a goodbye in Spain.

"Goodnight, and thank you again for dinner," Fi said. She wandered into the hotel, content with the evening and the fact that Luis was such a pleasant client. All in all, she was looking forward to her time in Spain.

CHAPTER 28

"So, how was your big date last night?" Liam asked when Fi strode through the shining glass lobby doors the next day. He looked as striking as ever in a charcoal grey suitcoat, a white button-down, and neatly pressed jeans. Today they would be touring the boat yard and some of the vessels, so they had been instructed to dress more casually. Fi had followed the advice by wearing a shimmery blue tunic over skinny jeans tucked into butter-soft leather boots. She'd strung a few necklaces around her throat – some of Aislinn's work – and had her tote on her shoulder. Digging in the tote, she slid her sunglasses on her face and pursed her lips at Liam.

"Don't give me that pout," Liam laughed.

"It wasn't a date," Fi said.

"Mmhmm," Liam grumbled.

"It really wasn't. He is a nice client, and I think, easy to socialize with. In fact, he asked if I thought you'd like to join us for dinner sometime as well." Fi dipped her sunglasses down with her finger and raised an eyebrow at him.

"Did he now? Couldn't he just ask me that himself?"

"And I'm sure he will," Fi said on a little huff of air as he got into the taxi that had pulled to their side.

"I'll reserve my judgment then," Liam said. "But you'll let me know if he tries anything with you?"

"And why would I do that? Are you my protector all of a sudden?"

"I've made it clear to you that I have an interest in you, haven't I, Fi?"

"That sounds like a *you* problem," Fi said, and smiled when Liam tossed his head back and laughed.

"Ach, woman, you're cold-hearted," Liam said, holding his hand to his heart.

"It's a difficult line to walk in business, Liam. Women deal with this every day. It's trickier in countries where men flirt as easily as they take their next breath. I want to walk the line of being friendly, but also not invite advances. It's not always easy doing so. Which is why I will push Luis back if he makes an advance – and why it's important to me that *you* also respect my boundaries while we are working."

"I absolutely respect your boundaries at work," Liam protested, and Fi had to agree. He'd been nothing but respectful during their business meetings yesterday.

Fi angled her head at him. "But it's after work we're discussing?"

"I enjoyed our dinner the other night. Even if it is only as friends. We've a past – you can't ignore that. You are aware of my interest. How do we handle that on this trip?

Can we not have dinner? Can we not see each other outside work? What are your rules?"

"I didn't say we can't go to dinner."

"Are you playing games with me, Fi?"

"No." Fi threw up her hands in frustration. "I'm horrible at playing games. I'm horrible at dating and all the dancing around and the nuances. I thought I was doing something right by being straight with you about everything and now it feels like I'm in the middle of something messy."

"It's not messy. But feelings aren't black and white. You can't be saying you don't feel anything for me, Fi." Liam patted her hand, making her turn to survey him through her sunglasses.

"Liam, now is not the time nor the place to be having these types of conversations," Fi said, pulling her hand back as the taxi rolled to a stop at the boatyard.

"It's a simple yes or no," Liam said, a stubborn look crossing his face.

"It's complicated," Fi sighed.

"It doesn't have to be," Liam countered.

"It does. Because that's me. I'm complicated."

"All right, then uncomplicate it for me. Tell me your rules and I will respect them."

"Just… okay, yes, we can have dinner and spend time together. But, truly, I'd like to keep it as friends. I'm not ready to explore further – especially during a contract negotiation as high-stakes as this one. I think it's best we don't have too much to distract us, no?"

"Aye, I can agree on that. And I'm sorry if I've pushed

you. I'll admit to a bit of jealousy when you went to dinner with Luis last night."

"I promise it was all on the up and up. And that's where I'll be leaving it as we're starting our workday," Fi said. She smiled as Luis and another man approached the taxi.

"Good morning, Fiona and Liam. I'd like you to meet Jonathon. He oversees much of the shipyard and will be touring with us today," Luis said, stepping back so they could shake Jonathon's hand.

Shaking off the conversation from the taxi, Fi focused on the words that flowed around her and did her duty, translating everything that was said. The hours flowed by easily as they toured the boatyard while Luis explained shipping routes and their environmental practices. It was interesting to Fi to learn about all the ins and outs of running such a massive operation, and she enjoyed her time tromping around the different ships and learning about how things were run. But by the end of the day, she was ready to put her feet up and relax – alone, as she'd promised herself.

"Fiona," Luis called as their taxi pulled up at the end of the day.

"One moment," Fi said to Liam, not caring that he gave her a look, and stepped away to speak to Luis.

"Do you have plans for dinner this evening? Perhaps I can take you and Liam out for a meal," Luis asked, nodding to Liam.

"Thank you for the invitation, but I will be eating alone tonight. I'm tired. I can see if Liam is free though," Fi offered, turning to wave her hand at him.

"Ah, well, then get your rest. I will try again later this week," Luis said, and stepped back, giving her a smile and a small nod. Fi noted he didn't offer to take Liam to dinner, but decided to let it go.

Liam was largely silent on the ride home and Fi found herself grateful for the peace. Translating could be exhausting work as she had to switch between languages in her head all day long. Content to sit in silence for a moment, Fi leaned her head back and watched the city go by.

"Would you like to grab a bite later?" Liam asked when they rolled to a stop at their hotel.

"I'm having a 'me' night," Fi said. "I just want to relax and read my book."

"Sounds like the perfect night. I enjoy cozying up in a hotel room and reading as well," Liam said. "Have a nice evening."

"Thank you, Liam," Fi said, smiling at him, her feet already aching from the heels she'd worn all day. A nice tub and a cozy bathrobe called to her.

An hour later, blissfully ensconced in her hotel robe and having enjoyed a glass of wine to unwind, Fi stared balefully at her door after a knock sounded.

"I swear... can I just get one night?" Fi wondered. After making sure the sash was tied tightly around her waist, she opened the door a few inches.

"Room service, madam." A waiter in a smart grey vest had a table on wheels loaded with plates in front of him.

"Oh. My apologies, but I didn't order room service."

The waiter checked his notepad.

"Fiona?"

"Yes, correct."

"This is for you from a Mr. Liam Mulder."

"Ah," Fi said and stepped back, allowing the man to enter. With efficient moves, he soon had the entire spread set up on the small table near the window, along with opening the bottle of wine, and even making sure the single rose in its clear blue vase was positioned just so. Thanking him, Fi closed and locked the door before moving to the table to pick up the small envelope there. Thumbing the flap open, she pulled out a note.

I didn't want to interrupt your alone time, but thought we could "dine" together in our separate rooms. Dinner's on me. Enjoy!

For a second, Fi's mind flashed to eating dessert off of Liam and a flush of heat touched her skin.

"Get your mind out of the gutter," Fi said, and then glanced over when her phone rang. Picking it up, she saw it was Grace and put her on video chat.

"Hi Grace, how are you?" Fi asked, propping the phone on the table and sitting down to look over her food options.

"What are you doing?" Grace asked, sitting at her own table in her cottage. Fi could see bowls and jars surrounding her and figured Grace must be working on her product line.

"Sitting down to room service dinner," Fi said, reaching out to take a sip from the glass of red wine the waiter had poured.

"Fancy. How's the trip going then?"

"It's good. Barcelona is nice," Fi said, knowing full

well that Grace must have heard Liam was on the trip by now.

"Is it? I've never been. And... work? It's good?" Gracie asked, her eyes wide in her face.

"Yup, all good," Fi said, taking a bite of cheese from the plate. "Dylan should be happy with this choice. The boatyard seems very well-run."

Gracie batted that away with a flick of her hand.

"And everything else? It's good?"

"Of course, why wouldn't it be?" Fi said, enjoying herself now as Gracie's face grew stormy.

"Just asking is all. I want to make sure you're not lonely traveling in these cities by yourself."

"Weird; you've never called and asked if I was lonely on my other travels," Fi mused, leaning back to kick her feet up on the other chair. "I can't imagine why you're checking in only a few days after I've last seen you."

"Because you're my best friend and I love you?" Gracie asked.

"Uh-huh. And this wouldn't have anything to do with a certain handsome Irishman who is also on this trip, would it?"

"What? What Irishman? Who could that be?" Gracie frowned and tried to pretend innocence. Fi almost spat out her wine.

"Gracie, you've never been able to lie for shite, and you know it."

"Damn it, Fi. Tell me! How are you and Liam? What's happening? Did you shag him yet?" Grace all but squealed into the phone.

"Oh, it's Liam you're asking after? Not the hot Spanish president of the shipping yard?"

Gracie drew in a long breath.

"You're playing around with two men?"

"I most certainly am not! You know I'm not like that. I don't have the wiles to do that. I'm too direct." Fi shrugged. "But I did have dinner with Liam. And I also had dinner with Luis. And I've made it clear to them both that I'll conduct myself in a businesslike manner until said business is concluded."

"It's tough, isn't it?" Grace said, her face instantly compassionate. "Navigating those lines in the business world?"

"It can be, yes. I'm trying to just stay focused on what Dylan sent me here for."

"I'm sure he wouldn't mind if you have your own life after business hours," Grace said. "He's not a monster like that."

"I'm aware I can have a work and personal life," Fi laughed, and took off the cover of another plate to find a selection of cured meats.

"How is Liam?"

"He's fine. I think he's making it clear he has an interest in me, but he's respecting my boundaries," Fi said.

"Why are you pushing him back?" Grace asked.

"I told you. It's all complicated. I like my life as it is, Gracie. Men complicate things."

"They don't have to. Sometimes they enhance things," Gracie said.

"I don't need enhancing. It's already a huge step for me

to have my own flat. Adding a man into the mix sounds too…"

"Restricting?" Grace asked, mixing something in a small bowl in front of her.

"Aye, that's a good word. You'll have to just let me muddle through this on me own." Fi sighed and then squinted when Grace held up the wooden stick she was holding in her hand. "What's that?"

"It's a muddle! I'm muddling an ingredient right now. So I'll be letting you muddle your way through this." Grace let out a peal of laughter. "Just know you can always talk to me about anything – you know that, right?"

"Of course I know that. I love you. Now, is your mum going crazy with planning?"

"Aye, the woman's enough to drive me mental."

he waves crashed far below where she stood on
the cliff's edge – angry, angrier than she'd ever
seen the cove. Dark clouds roiled on the horizon and a
sharp blast of wind whipped Fi's hair across her face,
blinding her for a moment. Pushing her hair back, Fi
studied the water that teemed at the edge of the beach.
What had made the cove so angry today?

When another blast of wind shook her, almost sending
her over the edge herself, Fi stepped back from the cliff's
edge just to be on the safe side. Shifting her gaze from the
storm rolling in to the waves below, her heart twisted when
a flash of brilliant blue shone from within the waters
before winking out of sight. She would have missed it had
she not been looking, and Fi shuddered as the punch of
magick rolled over her skin. She knew, instinctively, what
the light from the cove meant. She'd heard Grace tell of it,
as had other women in her family. But here, standing
alone? Why would the cove light for her?

Confused and uneasy with the electricity that thickened

the air, Fi turned from the water to walk back toward Grace's cottage, hoping to find a safe harbor there. She froze when she saw the two men standing at the cliff's edge.

Liam.

A smile on his face, he strode toward her, raising one hand in a hello. The wind threw his hair into tousled mess on his head, and he was several days past a shave. He looked handsome and at ease on the land, in a tartan flannel tucked under a simple grey wool jumper. He called to her, but the words were lost on the wind that tore across the land.

Did he see? Fi wondered, calling out to him. Luis walked behind him, and for a second Fi caught a wave of… *malevolence* washing from him. It appeared almost as if Luis was stalking Liam, like a cat about to pounce on a mouse – not like they were two colleagues having a stroll. Uncertain what this meant, Fi rushed forward with her hands in the air.

All she knew was she had to warn Liam – she had to save him! Her heart hammered in her chest and she shouted, the words lost on the shrieking gusts of wind that now pummeled them, and Liam stopped, his head tilted at her in confusion.

It was the last look she saw before Luis pounced, shoving Liam over the cliff's edge. The wind seemed to grab him and lift his body effortlessly as he plummeted from her sight.

"No!" Fi screamed, but the wind took her words, much as it had stolen Liam. She dropped to her knees in the wet grass as the clouds opened up, and sharp shards of rain pummeled her. Lifting her head, she saw Luis smiling at her through the mist.

Fi awoke with sweat dripping down her body and blinked into the pale light of the hotel room. Dragging in a shaky breath, she held her hand to her heart and forced herself to count her breaths until she could force herself to calm down. It took several moments before she could bring herself to shift in the bed and peel herself from the sweat-soaked sheets to stumble to the bathroom. Grabbing the glass next to the tap, she poured herself a drink of cold water and downed it, staring at herself in the mirror.

Dark circles smudged her eyes, and her skin, deathly white, held a sheen. Grimacing, Fi bent and splashed some water on her cheeks. Then she just sat – because she had to – on the edge of the tub and buried her face in the hand towel she'd grabbed.

She hated dreams like these, the ones where something awful was happening and she was left to decipher their meaning. Oftentimes, it could actually be the difference between life and death, and she'd learned over the years to understand which ones needed immediate action on her part and which ones were more metaphorical.

Yet this one was tricky. She couldn't imagine Luis actually trying to kill Liam. That was... laughable, Fi decided, standing up and moving to the shower to turn the water on. She waited as the water warmed, then slipped off her sleep tank and panties and stepped under the stream. Appreciating the waterfall shower head, Fi sighed as the heat loosened the tension in her shoulders. She braced her hands on the wall, letting water run down her back and soothe her muscles.

Was it simply trying to show her that Luis wasn't good for her? Or that he had ulterior motives? Or was her gift playing tricks with her mind? There was no handbook on something like this, no rules she could consult, and the last thing she was going to do was wake up any of her family in these pre-dawn hours. Deciding to push the dream away to take out and examine later, Fi spent longer than necessary in the shower before wrapping herself in the plush robe once more and padding out to her room. There, she brewed coffee and settled into the chair, forcing herself to read the papers for the day.

Routine soothed her, and within minutes, her mind had focused on translating the Spanish news and the dream was forgotten.

CHAPTER 30

They had a rare afternoon off the next day, and with the weather cooperating, Liam coaxed Fi into a walk down by the waterfront. The dream from the night before still lingered with her, but she'd spent the morning highly focused on Luis and had not been able to read anything untoward in his demeanor. Pushing it away as nothing more than a dream – after all, not all of her dreams were premonitions – Fi watched the sun playing on the water and the lazy swoop of the gulls overhead.

"It always feels like home," Liam said, taking a deep breath of the sea air.

"Aye, it does at that, doesn't it? I think if you've grown up around or on water, you'll always be drawn to it."

"I always say that I get land legs," Liam said, stopping by a small gelato stand and gesturing to it. Fi nodded; a gelato on a warm afternoon sounded perfect.

"Land legs?"

"Yes, I get itchy when I've been on land too much."

"I suppose I get the same when I've been in one spot

too long," Fi said, and then paused to peruse the gelato flavors. She decided on her go-to choice, pistachio, and laughed when Liam raised an eyebrow at her.

"What? Pistachio is delicious. You haven't tried it?"

"No, it's green. Gelato should be decadent looking, like this salted caramel." Liam gestured with his cone.

"Mmm, I'm thinking you might be changing your mind after a taste," Fi said, offering Liam her cone. Bending, Liam licked her gelato, and a shock of lust seared Fi's core. Despite her best efforts, her mind shot back to their night all those years ago in Croatia and memories of just what he could do with that mouth. Blushing, Fi turned away to look out at the water while Liam considered her gelato choice.

"Well, I'll have to be honest here – it's not bad. It's no salted caramel, and I can't say I'll be waking up in the middle of the night craving pistachio gelato, but it's not as bad as I was thinking."

"Do ye wake up in the middle of the night craving sweets often?" Fi laughed, grateful her momentary lust had subsided.

They continued down the cobblestone pathway by the water. Here, people clustered together in small groups, enjoying street food or biking past on their way to university. The crowd was a blend of tourists, businesspeople on their late lunch, or students with backpacks chattering in groups. Spying a rare empty bench, Liam dashed over and commandeered it before anyone else could take the spot. Settling on the bench, he waved her over before devoting himself to his gelato with a single-minded focus that made Fi smile.

"I'd be a liar if I didn't say that I've awoken a time or two with a craving for something sweet." Liam shrugged one muscular shoulder.

"I'll admit, I have similar moments," Fi said with a laugh.

"Duly noted. Call Fi at three in the morning and woo her with pistachio gelato." Liam pretended to write a note and Fi laughed again, stretching her legs out in front of her. She watched a container ship being loaded in the harbor and her mind drifted back to work.

"Do you enjoy this part of the job? The negotiations, that is?" Fi asked, savoring another mouthful of her gelato.

"Mmm, yes and no. I'm good at it, as I've a mind for details. But being good at it and loving it are two different things, no?"

"Sure, I feel the same with my work."

"You don't love translating?" Liam asked, turning to look at her with surprise.

"I do... but the business translations aren't what I enjoy," Fi admitted, amazed to be telling him this. She'd never even spoken the thought out loud before.

"But isn't that most of what you do?"

"Aye, it is. But... I don't know." Fi shrugged a shoulder and then took another bite of her gelato.

"Out with it, Fi. What would you rather be doing? You seem to light up when you're translating, so I'm surprised to hear you don't like it."

"Oh, I love it. The business contracts just don't excite me. If I'm to be honest... can I tell you what I'd really love to do?"

"Please," Liam said, leaning back so his shoulder bumped hers companionably.

"I think I'd like to translate books for a living. Fiction – novels, to be specific. Grand sweeping romances, cold murder mysteries, psychological thrillers – I think it'd be great fun. Maybe I wouldn't be able to travel as much, but I could travel on me own dime, couldn't I?" Fi demanded, warming to her subject. "And now that I have the flat, I could see myself working from there. Looking out over the water and translating books, then taking off for a holiday."

"I think that sounds wonderful, Fi. Why don't you do that?"

"Because… well, it's not what I went to uni for. I have a degree in business. That's what I should focus on."

"Why? I have a degree in business as well, but I prefer getting my hands dirty and building things or being at sea. I still use my degree when I need to, but I'm happiest when I'm doing physical things."

Fi's mind immediately flashed to a very naughty place and heat flushed her face. She hoped he wouldn't notice, and trained her eyes out on the water.

"I… uh…" Fi cleared her throat. "I don't think I've ever given myself permission to really explore what that path would look like."

"You should. It's what I've done with working for Dylan. He knows I'd go crazy if all I did was sit in a boardroom negotiating contracts all day. Instead, we've agreed I can have my hands in all levels of the business. I'm happy as a pig in shite getting dirty on a worksite or running a vessel through a storm at sea. It's good to have balance. Do you feel you have something to prove?"

Fi looked down to see she'd eaten all of her gelato. "I guess I do. I've always been so focused on getting out and exploring the world and proving I can be a strong businesswoman – I don't think translating novels fits with that image."

"Why not? It's a business. A very lucrative one, I imagine. I'm betting you'd be quite good at it as well. Why not give it a go?"

"I just might, at that. I'll think about it."

"Want to go to a museum with me?" Liam asked, standing up.

"What?" Fi forced her brain to change directions. The man had cut straight to her secret life dream, told her to go do it, and now he had bounced to visiting a museum?

"A museum? There's a Picasso museum here. I booked some tickets. I've never seen a Picasso. I think it'd be nice to add that to my list. Unless you've already seen a Picasso?"

"Actually, I haven't."

"Great! Should we both do something we haven't done before then?"

"I think we should." Fi laughed and stood, enjoying Liam's easy company and the fact that he'd kept his word not to push her. Being with him like this was as simple and as uncomplicated as hanging out with any of her friends.

If she ignored the stabs of lust that rocketed through her every so often, that is.

"Perfect. Shall we explore?" Liam offered her his arm.

She took it and, without a care in the world, took off for a wander with her friend.

CHAPTER 31

*T*he next few weeks sped by quickly. Fi's days were filled with translating business meetings and contracts, and her nights split between dining with Liam and Luis, or alone. True to his word, Liam had kept everything professional with her, and Luis hadn't overstepped any boundaries. She sensed his interest more than a time or two, but he hadn't made a move in that direction.

Luis was the type of man she'd typically have dated on her travels – slick, smart, and not interested in anything long-term. With no fear of attachments or feelings getting hurt, he'd be an ideal partner for a little fling after work was concluded.

Liam, on the other hand, was something altogether different. He… bothered her, in ways that she wasn't remotely ready to examine. Maybe it made her a bit of a coward, but if she had the choice between simple uncomplicated fun and messy emotional attachments, Fi was going to choose simple. It was just easier that way, Fi reminded herself – no messy attachments, no issues with

WILD IRISH DREAMER 197

overlapping friendships. She could easily see herself having a whiskey with Liam at the pub after Grace's wedding and not having any issue with him. But if they tangoed in the sheets? There would be issues. Fi didn't like issues. It was part of what made her dearly love traveling. She could love 'em and leave 'em and go on to explore the next place. Nobody got hurt, and everybody knew the score. With Liam, the truth of it was, she feared she would hurt him. Whatever was simmering beneath the surface between them was too potent – too large – to leave either of them unaffected. For her, it just wasn't worth having a taste.

"Where is this special place you're taking me?" Fi asked, smiling at Luis as she joined him outside the hotel. He'd invited her for dinner alone, as they would be dining together for their last night of work tomorrow.

"It is for fun. You'll enjoy yourself, I promise," Luis said, joining her in the back seat of the car.

"We're almost done with the negotiations, no? Tomorrow should finish everything," Fi said, stretching her legs out. Tonight she wore a flowing red skirt that stopped mid-calf and a simple black scoop-neck top. In lieu of necklaces she'd hung long silver dangles at her ears and had her Chanel bag on her arm. She'd learned quickly she'd never compete with the Spanish women Luis hung around, so instead she dressed how she felt most comfortable.

"I believe so." Luis looked away and then back to her, a smile stretching his handsome face. "And then... maybe we could spend some time together, if you stay on."

Fi paused for a moment. She wasn't entirely surprised

by his question, as she'd sensed a bit of interest from him. However, this was the first time he'd been direct about wanting something more with her.

"Not likely." Fi laughed at the crestfallen look on his face. "We're getting close to my friend's wedding, so I won't be staying much longer."

"Ah, but you travel frequently, no? We can plan around such things."

"Perhaps. I have had some inquiries on various projects, so I'll review the offers in the next few days and get a better idea on what's coming up next for me."

"Any projects in Spain?"

"I believe there were one or two. I *am* a Spanish translator, after all," Fi said with another laugh as the taxi rolled to a stop in front of a building with a line of torches on the balcony outside.

"I like this news. We can plan for a future date. Maybe someday you will take me to one of those craft markets." Luis smiled as he held out a hand and helped her from the car. Fi immediately dropped his hand once they were on the sidewalk, and she looked curiously at the building.

"Is this a restaurant?"

"Yes, a restaurant, bar, and dance club. Come, come. You'll see," Luis said, motioning her inside as he waved to someone across the way. They entered a room with a wide-open dance floor, already teeming with couples who were swaying to the music. Tables hugged the edges of the dance floor and a long bar dominated one wall of the room.

"Is this... are they doing the tango?" Fi clapped her hands in delight.

"We do many dances here. Tango, salsa, and free-form dancing. But yes, right now, there is tango."

"Oh, how fun, I'll love to watch. Thank you for bringing me." Fi followed Luis through the crowd until they reached a table tucked into the corner of the dance floor.

"Watch? Surely you'll try a dance?" Luis said, nodding to the waiter who appeared with a bottle of red wine in hand.

"Me?" Fi laughed and shook her head, caught up in watching the complicated movements of the dancers. "It's a very intricate dance. It would take ages to learn the steps."

"They have beginner dances. We'll try."

"Mmm, I'm not sure. Let me have some of this lovely wine and maybe liquid courage will help me." Fi laughed again, her eyes stuck on the movement of the dancers. They moved so well together, the delicate steps looking fluid and flawless as they executed the dance. Fi, caught up in the moment, stood and clapped when the dance finished. Luis smiled up at her.

"See? You have a passion for it. That is all that is needed. I promise," Luis said, squeezing her hand.

"Maybe," Fi said, sitting back down and glancing at her outfit. "At least I'm dressed for it."

"You look lovely this evening. But you always look lovely. You're a fascinating woman, Fiona." Luis never called her Fi, she realized, but always Fiona.

"You're very sweet," Fi said and then turned her eyes back to the dance floor, riveted as a new set of dancers took to the floor. Over an hour later, with two glasses of wine in her, Fi finally broke down and accepted Luis' invitation to dance when they called for a beginner round of dancers.

"I suppose, if we're all beginners, people will be kind to us?" Fi asked.

"Of course. We like when people try things. It is important to live life with a passion. Why sit on the sidelines? You'll make mistakes, of course. But you'll also learn."

"Tell me what to do," Fi said as Luis tugged her onto the dance floor.

"I will lead. Don't worry about the fancy footwork for now. Just get into the rhythm and twists. Fancy footwork comes much later in learning," Luis said, placing a commanding hand at her waist. Fi nodded and took a deep breath, focusing on the beat of the music when the song swelled around her. Following Luis' lead, she let him hold her close and together they twirled around the floor. She didn't stumble as much as she'd expected – with years of Irish dancing under her belt she could be quite light on her feet. By the time the song drew to an end, Fi was flushed and smiling. She caught Luis' intention right before he tried to kiss her and quickly turned her head so that his lips landed on her cheek. In doing so, her eyes locked on a familiar pair next to her.

"May I have this dance?"

"Liam," Fi said, pulling back from Luis. "I didn't know you were coming here."

"Nor I you," Liam said, nodding a hello at Luis.

"I just tried tango. I think I did all right, no?" Fi beamed over at Luis who smiled down at her.

"Of course. You were a delight," he said.

"May I have this dance?" Liam repeated, completely ignoring Luis.

"Certainly. I think I'm ready to try this again," Fi said. She kept her tone light, cutting through the tension that seemed to fill the air between the two men. For a moment, her mind flashed back to the dream she'd successfully ignored. The music began before any of them could speak again, and Liam whisked her to the middle of the dance floor.

"Have you tangoed before?" Fi asked, deciding to keep the conversation light. She didn't want to ask if he'd followed her here tonight.

"Believe it or not, I have." Liam smiled down at her and wrapped an arm around her waist. His nearness had an entirely different effect on her than Luis' had, and her stomach flipped in knots. Holding her eyes with his own, he dipped his head closer to hers, and for a moment she thought he might try to kiss her. "Luis is not the only man here with moves."

With that, Liam twirled her out and away from him, her skirt swirling in an arc around her legs, and Fi lost herself to the music and the dance. Every time Liam pulled her near, her pulse picked up, and by the time they ended the dance, they were both panting, their eyes locked on each other's. Fi took an unsteady breath, and then another, before stepping lightly back from Liam.

"Thank you for the dance. Please, won't you join us at our table?" Fi asked.

"I believe I will," Liam said. "Though I don't want to be out much later; we've a big day tomorrow."

"I agree," Fi said, returning to their table.

Luis stood on their arrival. "Ah, Liam, will you be joining us?"

"Just for one drink and then to the hotel. We've much to cover tomorrow," Liam said simply, and Luis nodded his head in agreement. Another glass was procured and soon the three sat at the table sipping their wine and admiring the dancers. Though the conversation was light, touching on the history of the dances they watched, Fi felt as though the tension had thickened in the air around them. Finally, annoyed with it all, she pushed back her chair to stand.

"I'm ready to go home. I'll just grab a taxi to go back to the hotel. Thank you, Luis, for a lovely evening."

"But – Fiona, I can take you."

"Really, it's fine. Finish your wine and your meal. I'm just tired," Fi said, stepping back from the table.

Liam rose. "I'll go back with you. I need to look over a few things."

Mentally, Fi groaned. She knew what it would look like to Luis, but found that she actually didn't care. The emotions at the table were messing with her head, and it was time for her to clear out before she did something stupid like let down her shields and read their minds.

"Please see her home safe," Luis said, as if he were allowing Liam to escort her.

"Naturally," Liam said, his smile more a baring of his teeth, and then they were gone.

A taxi waited conveniently out front and Fi dropped into it, grateful to be out of the dance hall and more than ready for bed. Emotionally charged situations were draining for her, and this one had too many elements for her to decipher.

"Fi…" Liam began, and she turned her head, simply looking at him. He caught her glance and shut his mouth, seeming to innately understand her need for silence. Instead, he reached out and squeezed her hand once before letting it drop.

Why she felt bereft at the loss of his touch was a question Fi didn't want to examine further.

CHAPTER 32

The next morning, the uneasy feeling stayed with her, but Fi did her best to push it aside and focus on her work. Today was the big day – the final translations and the signing of a multi-million-euro contract. Fi had finished all the contract translations and passed them over to Liam; however, she had been told there would be a few more changes to the clauses after further negotiations today.

As the afternoon drew late, Fi paced the small conference room at the boatyard where they'd stashed her to be available to finalize any information. Fi found it a bit odd that they hadn't asked for her in the last round of negotiations, but it seemed Luis felt confident enough in his English to handle the discussion. For now, Fi simply waited, as was her job, and hoped they'd wrap things up soon enough.

She'd promised Grace she would be home by this weekend, so despite her telling Luis they might have time for a date when business was over, Fi was likely to book a flight for tomorrow. She always waited to book her flights until she knew that a contract was officially signed and business was closed; she'd seen more than her fair share of deals fall through at the last moment. It didn't matter to her one way or the other if a deal went through, but she often felt bad for the people who had spent months negotiating only to come to an impasse.

The door opened, and Fi looked up and smiled when Luis entered carrying a laptop with him.

"Hello, Fiona. You are well?" They'd barely had time to speak today, so Fi nodded at him and smiled.

"I am well, thank you. How are negotiations?"

"I think this will be the last of it. Just a few things to change, which I've highlighted in red in the document."

"That's good to hear. I'll look over this and finish it up for you," Fi said, taking the laptop from him. She got a little buzz in her head when her hand touched his, and caught herself glancing at him.

"Yes?" Luis asked, catching her look.

"Oh, nothing." Fi shook her head, but the uneasy feeling still held and she almost – almost – dropped her shields and read his mind. Shocked that it had even flashed across her mind to do so, Fi blinked at the screen and forced herself to focus. This was a business arrangement, and really the last place she should be trespassing on someone's thoughts. What did it matter anyway? Luis had made it clear to her that he liked her; there was no need to violate the man's privacy just to assuage her doubts.

When she finished, Fi handed the computer back over.

Luis straightened from where he'd been checking his phone against the wall. "All done?"

"Yes, that should be the last of it."

"Wonderful. The car is out front to take you to your hotel." Luis held up his phone to indicate he had requested it.

"Should I wait for Liam?"

"He'll likely be another hour or two. You can wait, of course. But I suspect you'll be more comfortable in your hotel. Tonight we celebrate, yes?"

"I'm sure we'd all enjoy that," Fi said.

"Of course, of course. Dinner on me this evening. Until then," Luis said and left the room. Fi gathered her purse and looked around to make sure she'd left nothing behind. She still couldn't shake the uneasy feeling that had hung over her shoulders all day, but with nothing left to do but return to the hotel, she did as she was instructed. Once there she decided to indulge in something she rarely took the time for – a nap.

When she woke, blurry-eyed and confused, Fi blinked at the darkness around her. It had been light when she'd lain down, and clearly, she'd slept much longer than planned. Surprised that her phone hadn't rung to wake her, Fi picked it up from where it charged on the bedside table.

"Nine!" Fi said, shocked at the time. Typically, she would be meeting Luis or Liam for dinner by now, yet there were no messages on her phone. She decided to just call Luis, and waited while it rang before eventually going to voicemail.

"Hi Luis, this is Fiona. I'm just checking to see what

time dinner is for tonight," she said, glancing down at the robe she'd fallen asleep in. With any luck, she'd have time for a quick shower. "Just shoot me a text message and let me know. I'm going to hop in the shower."

She sent a similar message to Liam, assuming he would know about dinner as well, then waited a few minutes. When no response came, she shrugged and made a beeline for the bathroom. Enjoying the shower, she hummed to herself as she dried off, her thoughts on Grace's wedding next week. There was still loads to do, but she was grateful she'd have a whole week to help Gracie with all the finishing touches. When a knock sounded at her door, she grabbed her robe and wrapped it around her, pushing her hair back from her face.

"Yes?" Fi asked, easing the door open an inch. Seeing it was Liam, she unhooked the chain and opened it further. Her mouth dropped open when he shoved the door open and slammed it behind him to pace the room.

"Liam!" Fi said, censure in her tone as she studied the man who now prowled her room. His face was a storm cloud of fury and his shoulders hunched like he wanted to punch something. If ever she'd seen an angry man, this was one.

"*You,*" Liam bit out and then turned away from her to stare out the window at the city lights below.

"Liam, what's happened? You seem so upset. Tell me," Fi said, moving across the room to put her hand on his arm. She gasped when he wrenched his arm away and when he turned, she took two involuntary steps back at the look on his face.

"You…" Liam's breath came out in shaky puffs.

"Liam, you're scaring me. Is somebody hurt? Is it Grace? Or Dylan? Please, tell me what's wrong."

"I didn't expect this from you. I guess I should have – as I've learned, some women can't be trusted," Liam said and let out a little laugh, shaking his head at himself as he paced.

"Excuse me?" Fi drew herself up, her eyes narrow as anger rushed through her. "Sure and you can't be saying what I think you're saying?"

"Oh, don't be pulling your high-and-mighty act with me, Miss Fiona. I might have fallen under your spell before, but I see you for what you are now."

"And what's that, Liam?" Fi said, her voice dangerously low.

"A liar."

Fi's mouth dropped open but no words could form. She simply stared at Liam in shock.

"I should have guessed it. I really should have. Oh, you played it so neatly, didn't you? *No, Liam, I don't want to mix business and pleasure. No, Liam, I promise we're just colleagues.* Please! What. A. Bunch. Of. Shite!" Liam barked, and Fi's back went up.

"It was not a bunch of a shite. You want to know what's shite? You are! Storming into my room to yell at me with no explanation?" Fi fisted her hands at her waist. "How dare you?"

"How dare I? How dare I, she asks!" Liam raked a hand through his hair.

"Yes, how dare you? You have no right to come in here

and accuse me of being a liar. None at all. Why won't you tell me what the hell is going on?"

"Oh, I love that you're trying to play as if you don't know what this is about. But fine, princess, I'll tell you – you're a master manipulator, aren't you?"

"To hell with you, Liam," Fi hissed, fed up with whatever game he was playing.

"Oh, and same to you, sweetness, same to you. I bet you didn't know that I have a back-up translator to read all the contracts, to ensure that everything we've signed is the same on both fronts."

"I'm not surprised. That's smart business." Fi shrugged a shoulder. "And?"

"And she discovered that the contracts didn't line up. Not only in the shipping clauses, but the costs of shipment and fuel. Really a small number when looking at it, buried underneath everything else, but calculated over time, it's going to put about an extra three million euros in your man Luis' pocket."

"What!" Fi said, her mouth dropping open again. "There's no way. I went over those contracts front to back."

"Nice try, sugar. I've been down this road before, remember?"

"Liam! What in the world are you talking about? How… you can't possibly think that I would do something like that! You're mental. I would never, ever, do something like this. *Ever*. The fact you even could imply that I would…" Fi trailed off at the look in his eyes.

For a second, doubt seemed to cloud Liam's face. Fi

just looked at him, willing him not to believe this of her. He had to know she wouldn't have done something like this.

"I... Fi, I know I may be jumping to conclusions, but what other explanation is there?"

"You don't trust me," Fi said, her heart cracking.

"I've been down this road before, Fi. You've always kept me at a distance – never letting me too close, never letting me all the way in. And now this? I can't take any chances. It's hard for me to see what's right. I have to protect Dylan. I can't risk letting my feelings cloud my judgment."

"At my expense? You give me no benefit of the doubt? I thought we were friends." Fi blinked back tears.

"This is business, Fi." Liam looked away, his face like granite.

"Aye, I see," Fi said, straightening her shoulders. "Let me call Luis. I'm sure there's an explanation for this," she said, making her voice as cool as his.

"Try it," Liam said, crossing his arms over his chest and leaning against the door.

Glaring at him, Fi crossed to her phone and picked it up, putting it on speaker. Dialing Luis, she let the phone ring and ring until his voicemail picked up. Fi tried again. And again. And then once more. Each time it went to voicemail.

"Liam, I'm sure there's a reasonable explanation for this."

"The only explanation I can see is that Luis swept you off your feet and you turned a blind eye." With that, Liam left the room, shutting the door quietly and leaving Fi shattered.

She kept trying to call Luis. When it finally set in that he wasn't going to answer her calls, Fi dropped to the bed and did the only thing she could.

She called Grace.

CHAPTER 33

"*H*e says he'll be here. As I'm sure you understand, there's a lot he has to deal with right now," Grace said, squeezing Fi's arm before crossing her kitchen to the tea kettle that screamed for relief on the stove. Fi commiserated with the kettle; she felt like screaming too.

"It's not my fault," Fi began, repeating the refrain she'd said over and over since Liam had stormed from her room yesterday. She'd booked the first flight out and, unable to reach Dylan, had gone straight to Grace. Aside from everything else – protecting her reputation, making sure Dylan's company would be okay, and smoothing things over with Liam – she needed to see Grace first. It was as important to her as her next breath that Grace knew Fi would never hurt her this way.

"That's quite enough of that, now, isn't it?" Grace whirled in the kitchen, hands on hips, and glared at Fi. "I understand you're upset. And I know this needs fixing. We'll hash it all out, together, I promise you that. But if you think for a second that I'd be doubting you or be best friends with someone who would pull an underhanded snake move like that – well, then I don't really think you've a very high opinion of me, do you?"

"I love you," Fi said, hearing the thunder roll in the distance. Grace's moods notoriously kicked up the weather, and it sounded like this time was no different. "I'm sorry this happened and I'm sorry Dylan's company is having to deal with this."

"He'll handle it. It's what he does. He's a good businessman, and he has a team of solicitors that can take over the world if need be. I'm more worried about you, Liam, and what all happened in Barcelona. I had such high hopes…"

"High hopes for what, Gracie?" Fi sighed, accepting the mug Grace handed her. She took a sip and almost spat out the liquid. Gasping, Fi fanned her mouth.

"I thought this was tea."

"It's a hot toddy. Seems a dash of whiskey is what's called for in this weather."

"You're the one who called the weather," Fi said, taking a cautious sip of the toddy.

"I didn't call it. It just happens to respond to my moods." Grace and Fi winced as lightning flashed close to the cottage and thunder shook the shutters. Rosie whined and buried her nose in her blanket on her dog bed. Deciding she needed some comfort in the form of puppy snuggles, Fi left the table and crawled onto the dog bed with Rosie. The dog happily curled onto her lap, and Fi stroked her fur while staring into the flames of the fire crackling from the stove in the corner. For a moment, her eyes caught a form in the worn wooden rocking chair across from the fire. Fi tilted her head, and when the chair moved subtly, she smiled for the first time that day.

"Fiona?"

"Aye, she's here. But the electricity in the air is making it tough for her to come through at full power. She wants you to know she loves you."

"I love you too, Fiona," Fi said, a sheen of tears covering her eyes.

"She also says stop crying. Chin up, fix this, and go get your man."

"What? She did not." Fi glared at Grace.

"Something close to that." Grace turned and began arguing with the empty chair. "Well, seeing as how I'm your interpreter, I can interpret as I want. Don't get mad with me, it's essentially what you said. I swear... you are a finicky old woman. Fine. Fine!"

Fi pressed her lips together when Grace turned to her again.

"Fiona says to trust that this path is taking you where you are meant to go."

"To financial and career ruin?" Fi wondered.

"Oh stop, no. To Liam."

"This is not about Liam," Fi said, stroking Rosie's soft ears. "This is about everything I have worked for in my life coming crashing down around me."

"Fine, let's take Liam out of it for a second. Even if everything did crash down around you, would that be so bad? Sometimes things shatter so you can put the pieces back together in a different way. It may not look the same, but the process will have taught you something."

"Doesn't sound all that fun, Grace."

"Life isn't fun. I mean, it can be, but not always. Tough stuff is just that – tough stuff. You don't learn by having it easy your whole life. It's when things fall apart that you see who you really are."

"A sniveling mess?" Fi said, hugging Rosie closer.

"Sure, right now. But that's normal too. You cry because you care. You should care. It *matters*. But once you're done crying, you get up and fix things."

"I'm nervous about Dylan," Fi admitted.

"Well, he's arrived, so no time left to be nervous."

"How do you know that?" Fi wondered, but Rosie had left her lap and was standing by the door. Grace had turned to watch the door as well, and her face lit up when Dylan walked through. He immediately went to her, embracing her even though he was wet from the rain, while Rosie danced at his feet and demanded attention.

"Where's Fi?" Dylan asked, bending to give in to Rosie's demand.

"On the dog bed." Grace pointed. "She thinks she's in the doghouse."

"Jesus, Grace, I was just sitting with Rosie is all. She's a comfort to me," Fi said and made a move to stand, but Rosie raced back over and plopped in her lap.

"Sit, sit. Rosie loves the attention," Dylan said, taking off his coat and hanging it on a hook by the door. Taking the towel that Grace handed him, he wiped off his face and hair before leaning to kiss her once more.

"I made you a hot toddy," Grace said, bringing a cup over to Dylan. He nodded his thanks and pulled a wooden chair over to the sitting area. Fi noticed he didn't sit in the rocking chair, and wondered if he did that instinctively or if he knew that Fiona sat there. Grace settled on a bench by the table and together they looked at Fi.

"Why don't you tell me what happened?" Dylan asked, his eyes patient and understanding, and Fi immediately burst into tears.

"I'm sorry, I don't usually cry over business stuff," Fi said, accepting the tissue Grace handed her. "It's just that it's you and it's Grace, and it really really matters to me what you think."

"I'll know better what to think if you can explain your side of the story," Dylan said, taking a sip of his hot toddy and raising an eyebrow at Gracie.

"What? I figured we needed a heavy hand with the whiskey."

"No comment," Dylan decided and put his mug on the floor at his feet. "Go on, Fi."

"I don't really know what to say, I was absolutely shocked when Liam barreled into my room and started shouting at me."

"That is very uncharacteristic, for him to respond like that. He's usually quite even-tempered. In fact, even more so when he's about to go for the jugular. Was there anything else that contributed to his reaction?"

Fi could see why he was good at business. He kept the conversation on track and asked questions in a non-accusatory manner.

"I think… well, it might be a mix of business and personal that clouded his judgment. Though to be fair, I tried to keep it business."

"Please explain."

"Well…" Fi sighed and looked down at Rosie while she stroked her soft fur. "Liam made it known that he had some feelings for me. And I said I thought it would be better if we were just mates."

"Why is that?" Dylan asked while Gracie scoffed and buried her face in her mug of whiskey.

"Kind of exactly like this. If we were to be working together and have friends together… it's all too complicated and a messy overlap. I didn't want that. I've worked really hard for my career and my reputation. I don't like to cross lines there."

"Did you say as much to Liam?"

"I did – and to his credit, he respected my wish. Of course we had dinners and explored Barcelona together, but aside from a few times where he pushed my boundaries – very gently, mind you – he was exactly what he had said he would be."

"Which was?"

"A friend and a business colleague."

"Tell me about Luis," Dylan said, and his tone sharpened there.

"That is also where things got a little muddied," Fi admitted, reaching for her mug to take a long sip of the hot toddy.

"Go on."

"Luis invited me to dinner a few times. But he kept things all business. It was only on the last night before our last day of work that he asked me for a date down the road. Once the work was concluded."

"Did he now? Sure and that's the first I'm hearing of this," Gracie grumbled, but shut her mouth when Dylan shot her a look.

"This isn't the first time I've been propositioned in business, nor will it be the last."

"But you left it at that?"

"I did. In fact, Liam showed up at the same restaurant that night and we shared a taxi home."

"Okay. Did you spend a lot of time with Luis?"

"We'd have dinner every other night or so, and the three of us had dinner together a few times. I also had dinners with Liam and some nights I dined alone. You understand how it is when you're traveling alone in other cities... it's nice to have a companion for dinner."

"I understand," Dylan said.

Grace narrowed her eyes at him. "Is that right? Do you have a lot of companions for dinner then?" she asked, and thunder rolled over them.

"Usually my male business colleagues," Dylan said, reaching back to squeeze Grace's hand. "She's talking about being lonely in a new city – not about romance."

"Correct. Though I did let Luis know I might be open to a date in the future."

"You agreed to go out with him?" Grace interjected.

"Sure, why not? He's typically the type of man I'd date –"

"A liar and cheat?" Grace asked.

"A successful businessman who travels and isn't looking for a long-term relationship," Fi finished with a look for Grace.

"I can't believe you didn't guess his intentions," Grace bit out, then pressed her lips together when Dylan shot her a warning look.

"Why don't you tell me about the last day of nego-tiations?"

"I went in to the shipyard, which was our routine. Basically, I just waited around the rest of the day. Luis had indicated I wasn't needed for the last bit of meetings."

"Did you find that odd?"

Fi thought back. "I think I did, a bit, as I'd acted as translator on all the other meetings. But it seemed like they pretty much had everything sewn up."

"And the changes he had you make?"

"He came into the room where I was waiting late in the day and handed me a laptop. All he asked was that I make the changes he'd highlighted in red. I didn't read the whole contract; my assumption was that those clauses were the last details being discussed."

"And were they related to shipping and fuel costs?"

"Aye, they were."

"It didn't strike you as odd?"

"I… I can't say. I don't know the business so I don't know what's a fair price or not a fair price. I don't know what shipping routes were discussed. It's hard for me to make a judgement call on that, especially as I wasn't in the last round of discussions."

"He isolated you for a reason," Dylan said.

"I suspect as much."

"How could you have not gotten any indication that he was lying? Come on, Fi!" Grace exploded.

Fi leaned back to look at her in shock. "I felt a little buzz of something uneasy going on, but how was I to know?" Fi countered.

"You felt uneasy? And did nothing?" Grace threw up her hands.

"What was I supposed to do?" Fi all but shouted.

"Read his damn mind, Fi! Goddess above, you've been given a gift for a reason. And you ignore it and ignore it and now someone I love has gotten hurt!"

Fi's mouth dropped open that Grace had revealed her innermost secret, and the shock that flitted across Dylan's face before he composed himself said all she needed to know. Thunder exploded above them as Grace stomped into another room of the cottage, slamming the door behind her. Rosie stood up and whined, leaving Fi's lap to stand by the closed door.

Fi closed her eyes and took a deep breath, trying to bring her hammering heart under control. When she opened them, she found Dylan studying her.

"So you're a mind reader, then?"

"Aye," Fi whispered, and her tears ran as the skies exploded in rage around the cottage.

"$\mathcal{T}$his wasn't her secret to tell," Fi said, standing and brushing her pants off.

"I'm well aware there are many secrets among the ladies of Grace's Cove," Dylan said, standing as well. "Your secret is safe with me."

"That's not the point – she shouldn't be blurting that out. To anyone," Fi said, furious that Grace was hanging this business problem on her not using her gift.

"I also understand that. Our Gracie can be a bit tempestuous at times," Dylan said, his lips quirking in a small smile when thunder rolled over the cottage again.

"It's not my job to use anything... *extra* in my business dealings," Fi said, her back stiff. "I can swear to you that I didn't know he was deceiving you. We never talked business when we were out. Despite Liam's accusations, I didn't string anyone along, nor did I manipulate anyone. I truly was shocked when he confronted me. I hope you can believe me."

"I do believe you, Fi. I trust my gut in my business

dealings. I also trust Liam but I think, in this instance, his own personal past may be clouding the issue for him."

Fi looked at Dylan for a moment before shutting her eyes.

"Of course. The woman he was going to propose to."

"Aye."

"He thinks I would lie and scheme just like her."

"I imagine that once he's cooled down, he'll see that's not the case."

"He doesn't think very highly of me then."

"Liam is very protective of me and our business dealings. Typically, he's very coolheaded, but it seems in this instance he's allowed personal feelings to cloud his reasoning."

"Which is exactly why I was trying to not be involved with him!" Fi threw up her hands. "This is exactly why! Now everything is messy. He thinks I'm a liar. Your business is screwed. Grace and I are fighting – everything's a mess. This is *exactly* why I didn't want to get involved with him."

"Well, I hardly think you could have predicted a bad business deal… unless you can tell the future as well?" Dylan smiled gently at her.

"She can!" Grace yelled from her bedroom.

"Oh feck you, Gracie!" Fi shouted and stormed to the door. Grabbing her coat, she leveled a look at Dylan. "I stand by my words. I'll speak with any authority or court that you need me to. Otherwise, I'm done here."

Without waiting for his response, Fi stormed into the rain that rocketed down in heavy sheets. Not caring that the rain hit her face like little shards of glass, she slammed the door of her car and turned the car toward the village. As she drove past the cove, Fi looked to the cliffs and bared her teeth.

"Screw you... stupid cove. Stupid magick. Stupid gifts," she chanted. Rolling her eyes as lightening flashed over the cove, Fi continued her drive home.

Then her dream flashed before her eyes. In the dream, Luis had thrown Liam over the edge of the cliff. At the time, Fi had thought it had to do with personal issues. Now, she realized the dream had been telling her something entirely different.

"How would I have known?" Fi fumed. "Even if I had opened myself more, it's unconscionable to read people's thoughts."

Furious with everything and everyone, and deeply exhausted, Fi parked by her flat and stormed up the stairs. Why was she in trouble with everyone? She hadn't lied. She hadn't cheated. She hadn't revealed anyone's deeply personal secrets.

That last part burned.

For all the years that she and Grace had been friends, Fi could only remember one big blow-up, and it had been over a boy. Never something like this. Fi stripped off her wet clothes and pulled on comfy pants and a sweatshirt, pulling a blanket with her as she plodded to her window seat. Curling up, she watched the storm roil over the water. Despite their different approaches to magick and their gifts, Fi had always been able to trust Gracie.

Added to all of that, she couldn't be sure that Dylan wouldn't tell Liam about her extra abilities.

Fi groaned and buried her face in the blanket for a

moment as her mind raced. If Liam knew she could read minds, then he'd likely be even more certain that she'd betrayed him. Because the logical conclusion would be, why hadn't she read Luis' mind if he had given her an uneasy feeling? She might have been able to prevent what had happened if she had. For someone who had never lived with this ability, it would probably seem like the simplest answer. Someone puts you off? Read their mind. Find out their true intentions.

It wasn't that easy, but Fi couldn't imagine Liam being in any frame of mind to accept or understand that. Knowing she was well and truly screwed now, both with Liam and Gracie, Fi stared out the window as tears rolled down her cheeks.

Why *hadn't* she read his mind?

The question slammed into her and she took one long shuddering breath. Outside, the waves crashed into the shoreline as the wind ripped the rain across the street. The few people unlucky enough to have to go outside in this weather ducked their heads against the bracing wind and ran for their cars. In the sky, dark clouds hung like a thick blanket, illuminated from within by flashes of lightning. Oh, Grace was in a rare mood, that was for certain, Fi thought. She closed her eyes and leaned her head back, taking a few deep breaths and working to calm the turmoil that raged in her gut much like the storm outside.

"You're in quite the mess."

"Jesus!" Fi almost jumped out of her skin. She was grateful her window seat wasn't a balcony, or she would have toppled right over the edge. "Fiona, we talked about this."

"How else am I supposed to announce my presence? You want me to move some things in the room? Make a 'woooooo' noise?" Fiona asked, crossing her arms over her chest. Fi could see her more clearly now, though her image wavered a bit.

"Something to announce that you're in my flat would be nice, yes," Fi grumbled.

"I'm here," Fiona said, and waved at her.

"Yes, thank you, I can see that. And now the whole town will think I've gone crazy, sitting here in my window seat and talking to the wall."

"So don't sit in the window seat then." Fiona shrugged.

"It's comforting to me," Fi argued.

"Then you've got another dilemma on your hands."

"What do you want, Fiona?" Fi asked, not caring that she was being rude to a ghost.

"I wanted to see if you were all right."

Fi closed her eyes at the kindness in Fiona's voice, and willed the tears back. "I'm not in me best mind, and that's the truth of it," she whispered.

"So it seems. It's been a hard day."

"It has."

"I'll ask you the same question you just asked yourself. Why didn't or don't you use your gifts?"

"Why does everyone refer to them as gifts? What if they aren't gifts? What if they're chains?"

"You feel shackled by your gi– er… abilities?"

"It's not like I have the fun gifts. I can't do magick spells or make the weather bend to my mood. I can't make something float across the room to me. Hearing people's thoughts is the worst! And the dreams? Who wants prophetic dreams? They're almost impossible to figure out and when I do, sometimes it's too late anyway. Like in this case."

"You had a dream then?"

"Aye. I had a dream."

"Tell me about it."

"I was by the cove." Fi sighed and pinched her nose as she took herself back to the dream. "It was bad weather, like today. I was leaving and the cove flashed blue, which made me turn and look."

"Who else was in the dream?"

"Why do you think someone else was in the dream?" Fi asked.

"It's rare for the cove to shine its light for someone alone."

"Well, it was just a dream, so it could do what it wanted."

Silence greeted her and Fi sighed, tugging the blanket tighter around her as another blast of thunder shook the building.

"Liam was there. As was Luis. Luis snuck up on Liam and tossed him off the cliff."

"Ah."

"That's it? 'Ah'? I thought you were some mystical guidance counselor," Fi griped. "That's all you can say?"

"It's not for me to figure this out for you. You have to do the work," Fiona said, and Fi wrinkled her nose in distaste.

"What if I don't want to do the work?"

"Then I'd say you're sulking, being a child, and

refusing to learn or grow," Fiona said, her tone like a knife coated in honey.

"Can't a body have a good sulk once in a while?"

"Of course. But then it's time to figure things out."

"I haven't finished sulking," Fi said, pushing her lower lip out.

"How did the dream make you feel?" Fiona asked on a sigh.

"It made me feel… not great. I felt like it was telling me to protect Liam."

"And now?"

"I think it was warning me that Luis would betray us. And that I shouldn't trust him."

"Did you trust him?"

"I… well, I felt like I had a good reading on him, in the sense that I knew what he was about, especially if I ever went back to Spain and had a fling with him. He was safe."

"Why safe?"

"Because I wouldn't have to get my feelings involved."

"Ah."

"Don't 'ah' me," Fi said.

"Well, that says a lot, no? And Liam scares you."

"It doesn't matter what Liam does or doesn't do anymore. He's done with me. He made that clear."

"That's his temper. He owes you an apology, that's for sure. He'll come around. The man just needs a cooling-off period. I'm certain you can talk this through with him."

"Why bother?" Fi shrugged a shoulder. "He's judged me and found me wanting. I shouldn't have to explain myself to him. He's decided I'm a liar and a cheat."

"You can defend yourself."

"If he's that unwilling to trust me, I have no need to defend myself. I don't have to have a relationship with him at all."

"You'd think you'd be more understanding of someone who has been hurt badly before," Fiona said, making a clucking noise with her tongue.

"I haven't been hurt like he has."

"Haven't you? Are you forgetting Brian? Isn't that the entire reason you've never shown yourself to a man again? Never opened yourself? Liam's not necessarily wrong for not fully trusting you. You've held yourself back from him."

"I have to protect myself."

"You have to learn to trust. So does Liam. You can do it together."

"Doubtful." Fi shifted, tucking the blanket tighter around her feet.

"Perhaps a little compassion here might go a long way."

"Maybe, maybe not. Either way, I'll do what I can to be polite with him and that's that."

"Tell him who you are. Show him," Fiona insisted.

"Why? I don't use that side of myself."

"You should. It will help you."

"How? I don't need to know what Mr. Murphy is thinking at the end of the bar."

"If you'd take the time to hone your ability, you could use these things to your benefit. You'd be better at business negotiations, more helpful in warning others of trouble – even your dreams would make more sense. When you close yourself off from your power, you're diluting your contributions to this world."

"I –" Fi began, then looked around and cursed. The flat was empty, and she was left alone with her thoughts. Leave it to a ghost to get the last word in.

CHAPTER 35

Why Dylan had made him meet at Gallagher's Pub, of all places... Liam shook his head as he stomped down the sidewalk of Grace's Cove. Passersby correctly interpreted his mood and steered clear of him, some going even as far as to cross the street.

"Oi! Liam!" Mr. Murphy beamed at him from where he'd hobbled to the front door of the pub. "That's a nice lad, back in town. You're here for the wedding?"

Liam didn't have it in him to be mean to an old man, even if he was spoiling for a fight. He'd save his mood for Dylan, Liam thought as he held the door for Mr. Murphy.

"Aye, I am at that. Best man and all," Liam said.

"We're all looking forward to it. They sure know how to throw a bash," Mr. Murphy said, tottering over to his stool and clambering onto his seat as he'd done every day for thirty years. Liam squinted in the dim light of the pub, his eyes taking a moment to adjust before he scanned the room. Cait worked the bar and she nodded to him, but

Liam didn't see Dylan until he turned toward the dining area. There Dylan sat, cozied in a booth with Grace. Lovely, Liam thought; now he'd have to deal with both of them. In a vicious mood, he bypassed the bar and slid onto the bench across from Dylan and Grace.

"Liam." Grace nodded, her tone frigid. Liam raised an eyebrow at that and then turned to look at Dylan in question.

"Grace, be nice."

"Well, the man's made false accusations against my best friend," Grace sniffed, examining a chip in her nail.

"I thought you weren't speaking to Fi," Dylan said. "Now you're mad at Liam on her behalf?"

"I can be mad at the both of them at the same time. It's my wedding week, isn't it?"

"Ours, darling. It's *our* wedding week." Dylan laughed and squeezed her arm.

"You'd better fix this with Fi. I can't be dealing with this drama before the wedding." Grace narrowed her eyes at Liam. Never one to be cowed by an angry woman, Liam just lifted his chin.

"I don't have to be fixing anything, Grace. She's landed herself in her own trouble."

"Be that as it may, it's not for the reasons you're thinking," Grace began, but Dylan interrupted.

"Let's throttle back a moment. First, would you like a pint?"

"Of course," Liam said, and Grace slid from the booth to go get him a drink.

"Listen, Gracie is in a real snit about all this, so tread carefully, okay?"

"I am not in a snit," Grace said, materializing back by the table, her hands on her hips.

"Damn, you move like a cat. And I know a snit when I see one." Dylan held up a hand to stem the flow of words bound to come out of Grace's mouth. "Let's just hear what Liam has to say. First of all, how did it go in Spain?"

"The authorities were very cooperative. It appears they've had their eye on Luis for a while now due to various other shady business dealings, but they haven't had any ironclad proof. And this all lines up with my feelings about him all along."

"And the authorities are going to go after him?"

"Absolutely. I supplied them with the contracts we signed – I'd scanned them with an app on my phone when I signed them – and they were able to see the changes that were made after the fact. Unfortunately for us, he's left town."

"No idea where he is?"

"Monte Carlo's the word. They're working with the police there and hope to arrest him later today. If not, it's just going to take time to bring him in."

"What will happen to his company?" Grace asked. They looked up when Cait appeared with a tray with a round of drinks on it.

"Liam." Cait nodded, her tone stiff.

"Cait, nice to see you."

"I wish I could say the same for you," Cait said, and for a brief second, Liam feared she might dump the pint in her hand over his head.

"What did I do?" Liam demanded.

"My girl's up there, refusing to leave her flat. Because of you."

"It's not because of me – it's because she's mad that she got taken for a ride," Liam scoffed.

"Were you or were you not rude to my daughter?" Cait's voice had sharpened to steel.

Liam braced his shoulders. "I might have been rude, but I was protecting Dylan's company."

"Then you need to apologize."

"Me? I will do no such thing," Liam began, but Dylan interjected.

"Cait, I'm sorry to interrupt," Dylan said, wincing as her steely gaze speared him, "but I'm just getting the report on what the police had to say. We can get to personal once business is concluded, if you don't mind."

"I've got my eye on you," Cait said, pointing a finger at Liam before she stomped away.

"How have I become the bad guy here?" Liam held up his hands.

"Oh, let me count the ways," Grace began.

Dylan slapped his hand on the table, making her jump. "Stop. Seriously, stop. Business first."

"The owner of the company has fired Luis and is returning from his yacht in Greece. He's also cooperating fully with the authorities, and hopes that you'll still consider doing business once they've done a full audit of all employees. And he did mean all – from the top all the way down to the janitor who sweeps the floors at night. I liked him, for what it's worth. I think he was genuinely shocked by all this. He's grown lax with his company, getting on in age, and this was an eye-opener that he needs a firmer hand on the reins."

"I'll take that into consideration. Can you set up a meeting to discuss for next month?"

"I'll do that," Liam said, blowing out a breath and then taking a long sip of his drink. "Business concluded?"

"For now, yes."

"So," Grace began, but Liam held up a hand to shush her. A storm washed over her face, but he didn't care.

"I know I was harsh with Fi."

"You were horrible, from the sounds of it."

"I can be worse," Liam promised.

"That's not helping," Dylan whispered, then shut himself up at Grace's look. It was her turn to run the show.

"Do you honestly think that Fi has it in her to manipulate and cheat someone? Her best friend's fiancé? I'm shocked, honestly shocked, you would think that of her." Grace's expression turned to wounded on behalf of her friend.

"I understand your feelings," Liam began and held up a hand when Grace looked to interrupt him, "But I allowed personal feelings to mix with business. I wasn't thinking clearly when I exploded on her."

"You know Cait." Grace nodded to the bar. "You've seen how she runs this establishment. Do you think she would raise a liar of a daughter?"

"No," Liam sighed and pinched the bridge of his nose. "No, I do not. After I calmed down I realized that I may have made assumptions."

"She didn't know, Liam. Truly. She explained what happened – how Luis slipped into the room and asked her to change a clause. She didn't even understand what she was changing. Fi just thought it was a clause you two had discussed. She doesn't know enough about the business to even understand how that would have impacted the bottom line."

"I get that now." Liam sighed again.

"She's worked incredibly hard to build her reputation as a reliable and trustworthy interpreter. She works with high-level clients all around the world. Even a whisper of shady dealings could destroy everything she's worked for. Why would she put her life on the line like that?" Grace asked.

"I get it, I get it, I get it," Liam groaned. "Listen, a part of me just flashed back to when I found out I was being taken for a ride. My feelings... well, my feelings for Fi run deep. And it all overlapped and got confused in my head. I felt like I was being taken advantage of again. Like I couldn't trust my own instincts with women."

"It's not like that," Grace promised, this time reaching out to squeeze his hand. "I promise you."

"I've been an arse," Liam concluded.

"Make it right," Cait said simply, appearing over Liam's shoulder and making him jump. She brandished a key in front of Grace. "Both of you. You too, Gracie. You owe her an apology."

"I –!" Grace glanced at Liam and shut her mouth.

"What did you do?" Liam said, his eyebrows raised in surprise.

"None of your business," Grace griped.

"Now who's being a child?" Liam murmured, and jumped again when Cait snapped her fingers.

"Both of you. Now. Go make it right. Don't set foot in this pub until you do."

"But…" Grace said, looking to Dylan.

"He can stay. You two are officially kicked out."

Liam glared at Dylan's wide grin and slid from the table with Grace at his side.

"I feel like I just got scolded by my teacher."

"She's much scarier than a teacher. Do what she says," Grace whispered. Then, together, they hustled out of the pub to rescue Fi from her self-imposed prison.

CHAPTER 36

Fi started at the sound of her door opening and jumped up from where she'd curled, once again, on her window seat.

"Liam!" Fi gasped, instantly looking down at herself and then at Liam, looking gorgeous as ever, standing in her doorway. She hadn't showered in three days; she was certain she'd dropped some sort of food down her shirt – or were those coffee stains? – and hadn't put on deodorant in a while. Not her best look, Fi decided, but straightened her shoulders.

"You can't just barge into my flat, Liam. That's breaking and entering," Fi sniffed, even though her pulse picked up and her heart did a little bumpy shiver in her chest.

"Is it? Entering, maybe, but I have the key – given to me by your mum. So, I guess not technically breaking. Though I don't mean to scare you." Liam stepped inside and closed the door gently behind him. Leaning against the wall by the door, he crossed his arms and stared at her.

"That's it? You're just going to stare me down?" Fi fidgeted with the hem of her T-shirt, desperately wishing she could see what she looked like right now.

"I..." Liam cleared his throat. "It appears I may owe you an apology."

"Oh, is that right?" Fi said, sticking her nose in the air, though she feared any attempt at trying to look dignified was lost in view of her ratty sweatpants and fuzzy hot pink pig socks.

"Aye, that's right. It has come to my attention that perhaps you didn't actually know about Luis' fraud."

"*Perhaps* I didn't? Or actually I didn't?" Fi demanded.

"Actually you didn't."

"Correct. I did not. I would never, *never*, have hurt my best friend's fiancé that way. Hell, Liam, *any* company I worked for. I don't even have to have a relation to them."

"I'm sorry. Ah, Fi, I screwed up. I let my own feelings blind me and I just... I just saw red, I did. It takes a lot for my temper to boil over, but when it does... I just can't be seeing straight."

"You had no right, no right, to accuse me of what you did." Fi jabbed a finger in the air.

"I know. And I'm sorry, I am. I can only hope you'll forgive me. Will you accept my apology?"

"I can accept your apology," Fi said, shrugging a shoulder, "But I can't forget how you made me feel."

"Och, that's a sting to me heart," Liam said, rubbing his chest. He stayed where he was, correctly guessing that Fi wouldn't allow him close to her.

"You hurt me," Fi whispered, doing her best not to let

tears well up. "That you would think that? Of *me*? It's… awful. And you were so willing to believe I'd be that person. That hurts more than anything. I understand everyone makes mistakes. I truly do. But you believed that of me. Which means you don't really know me at all."

"You haven't given me much of a chance to know you, have you, Fi?"

"Oh, this is my fault, is it? Don't be trying to put this on me, Liam," Fi seethed, beginning to pace in the room as she warmed to the topic. "This is about your issues, not mine."

"I'd say it's both of ours." Liam held up his hands when she glared at him, "Fine. I'll start. You know how broken I was after my ex-girlfriend screwed me over. You know I was about to propose to her. It took me a long time to trust again after that – hell, I'm not sure I actually have fully trusted someone since then."

"I know she hurt you."

"And I thought… with you… well…"

"Well, what?" Fi crossed her arms across her chest, hoping to cover up most of the stains.

"I guess I saw myself being able to trust again. I liked that you didn't play games with me. You weren't coy or manipulative and you said things to me straight. I appreciated that in you. And… I like you, Fi. I genuinely like you."

"But you were willing to believe the worst of me."

"I guess, yeah. Because I did develop feelings for you. You scared me. The idea of you scared me. You're every-thing I've ever wanted in a woman, a partner, and a best friend. I want to be around you. Spend time with you. Travel with you. It's you that I want."

Fi's breath left in a whoosh.

"Liam…"

"I'm sorry I hurt you. I don't know if you'll be able to see past it or not, but I hope you can."

"I understand your ex-girlfriend did a number on you. But you can't hold everyone to that standard forever. You have to trust sometimes. And you don't trust me," Fi said sadly.

"And you don't trust me. Not enough to let me all the way in. Not enough to try and work this out," Liam shot back.

"That's not fair. This isn't about me – this is about you and your accusations."

"Maybe so, but you've always held yourself back from me. And if you truly can say you don't have feelings for me, that's fine, I get it. But you haven't been able to, and that's not fair to me either."

"You're not wrong. Maybe I have kept you at a distance. I wanted to avoid all this. Everything's a mess. I'm fighting with Grace. We're fighting. Dylan's in the middle. This is exactly what I didn't want to happen. The messiness of it all. It's why I always pick up and keep traveling and going… I'm not good with all these emotions and the back and forth. And it's Grace's wedding week! I should be there for her."

"So be there for her. Can we… can we work this out? Tell me what you need, Fi."

"I… okay." Fi took a breath. "I forgive you, Liam. But I need some time. This week shouldn't be about me. It needs to be about Grace and Dylan. I'm ready for us to go back to being mates."

"Just mates?" Liam asked.

"It's all I can give right now," Fi said, her heart cracking at the sadness that swept his handsome features.

"I'll respect your wishes then. There's, ah, someone else here who wants to see you."

Liam had barely said the words before Grace barreled into the room. Stopping, she wrinkled her nose at Fi's appearance. "Ew."

"I'll just be letting myself out now. Grace, you'll let me know if I can help with any planning this week. Fi, I'll see you at the wedding." Liam nodded, and with that he was gone.

When he left, Fi's heart dropped, and she felt his absence keenly in her flat.

"You look like a hot mess," Gracie said.

"Lovely, thanks for that," Fi said, wary of another emotionally-charged discussion.

"Did you mean what you said? That this week is supposed to be about us?"

"It is, yeah."

"Well then, why are you moping up here?"

"Um, because you betrayed my trust to Dylan?"

"Why are you so scared to show yourself to Liam? He's scared but he told you how he felt. He's right – you are a liar. You're lying to yourself and to him. He doesn't know the real you, and you've done that to yourself."

"If you consider that an apology, you've got some work to do," Fi said, her hands on her hips.

"Well? For feck's sake, Fi!" Grace exploded. "Stop

dancing around this! You have a good man out there. A man who will support you and partner with you. But you have to be honest with him. Stop hiding yourself from the world – from love – and live your damn life. It's a gift not afforded to everyone!"

"Again, your apology needs some work." Stubborn, Fi held her ground, though Grace's words made her stomach turn.

"Look, I'm sorry I told Dylan about you. I trust him with my life about… everything. He would never betray or hurt you. But you're right, it wasn't my secret to tell. That being said, you need to trust Liam. He knows about magick. He believes in it. He'll love you more for it, probably."

"I've never told anyone outside of our circle aside from he-who-shall-not-be-named," Fi whispered, turning away to return to her comfort spot in the window seat. "What if he hates me? What man wants a life with a woman who can read his thoughts?"

"Um, your father for one, duh." Grace shook her head at Fi and crossed to sit next to her. "Let's be honest – when you live with someone, when you love them, you can practically read their minds anyway. I promise you, if you give this a chance, you won't regret it."

"You can't know that. I'm the prophetic one, remember?" Fi said, leaning over to bump her shoulder against Grace's.

"And? I'm betting you've had a dream about this. What did it show you?"

At Fi's mulish expression, Grace threw back her head and laughed.

"I think that's all I need to know. Please don't be mad at me anymore. I need you this week."

"I'm not. I love you," Fi said. She went to hug Grace, who instead pulled back and wrinkled her nose again.

"Maybe after you've showered."

"Remind me why I'm your friend again?"

CHAPTER 37

*T*he wedding day had arrived.

The rest of the week had passed in a blur of preparation for Grace and Dylan's big day, and Fi had barely had time to talk to her own mother, let alone Liam. Oh, she saw him periodically, but it was always with a group of people around them. True to his word, he treated her as a friend and kept a respectful distance. Fi hadn't known the difference between Liam showing an interest in her and Liam just as a friend, but she found that she missed the Liam she knew. The Liam she had grown used to would throw her little looks, or smile at her periodically even when someone else was talking, and there was just an extra sparkle to his attention to her. Now, it was like someone had turned the light off and he was flat and polite with her.

Which was what she'd asked for, Fi reminded herself.

"Fi, it's your turn for hair and makeup," Grace called. Fi shook her head and headed into Grace's bedroom in the cottage which had become wedding central.

"Oh, Grace, you look lovely," Fi breathed. Grace's hair had been pulled half back in an intricate braid, with a ribbon woven through it. The rest was left to tumble down her shoulder, and a floral crown would complete the look once she was in her dress.

"Thank you. As will you. Do you think he'll mind that I've reversed the tradition?" Grace nibbled her lip as she eyed her dress where it hung on the wall. An ombre blush color, the dress had been hand-dyed so that the palest of pinks started at the bust and flowed through to a deep fuchsia layer at the hem. With miles of skirt tumbling around her, Grace would look like a wildflower sprung from the garden. For her girls, she'd chosen white, and Fi had to admit, their bridesmaids' dresses were stunning.

"I think the man will lose his mind when he sees you," Fi promised, then closed her mouth so the makeup artist could do her magic. It wasn't long before Fi was prepared and ready for her own floral crown, but first she had to slip into her dress. Sneaking away to the bathroom, she took off her robe and slid the simple white dress over her head. Grace had chosen well here, Fi thought as the cool silk slid over her body. With a simple halter neck, the gown hugged her body without being tight, and the simplicity of it only contributed to its elegance. When she walked out into the bedroom, Grace clapped her hands.

"You look amazing. Oh, Fi, you look like you're getting married."

"Hush, now, I do not. But I will say, you've picked a good dress."

"Let's put the crown on," Gracie instructed the makeup

artist, who dutifully clipped a crown of blush pink flowers entwined with greens to Fi's head.

"Does it look silly? It feels like it should look silly."

"No, I… wow," Gracie said, pointing to the full-length mirror. Fi walked over and studied herself. Her eyes looked huge in her face, darkened from the makeup, and her lips like a ripe raspberry waiting to be plucked. Though she'd never been a flower-crown person, she had to admit, it looked amazing with the simplicity of the dress.

"Sure and you did a lovely job putting this all together, Gracie."

"Now it's my turn!" Grace squealed. Not caring about modesty, she dropped her robe and stood by her dress while Keelin and Fi helped her into it. When they'd finished and Fi fluffed out the skirts, the room came to silence.

"Well?" Grace demanded.

"I can't speak, or I'll cry," Keelin said, both her hands to her face.

"No, don't ruin your makeup," Gracie ordered.

"You're a vision," Fi breathed. "Go look at yourself."

A wide smile broke out on Gracie's face when she stepped to the mirror. She looked lit from within, and happier than Fi had ever seen her. She would never forget this moment, Fi realized, for she'd always hoped her friend would find such happiness.

"It's time," a voice shouted from the front of the cottage and everyone flew into a flurry of activity – last-minute makeup touches, bouquets to grab, and last glimpses in the mirror. Finally, Fi stood at the front of the cottage where she was to meet Liam and walk out together. Apprehension stole through her. As best man and maid of honor, they had a lot of duties together tonight. Fi hoped she'd be able to keep the day focused on Grace, and not let her own emotions steal into it.

"Ready?" Aislinn asked, poking her head through the door of the cottage.

"Is Rosie set?" Gracie called.

"Aye, she's ready," Fi called back. As ringbearer, Rosie was decked out in a collar of flowers and ribbons, and from the way she pranced and wagged her tail, Fi guessed she quite liked all the attention.

"Let's make an honest woman of me then."

Fi laughed and stepped through the cottage door. For a moment, the light outside blinded her and she blinked to adjust her eyes. Liam stood, the expression on his face indecipherable, and simply stared at her.

"Do I look bad?" Fi said, looking down at herself and then up at him. He shook his head, as if in a fog, and cleared his throat.

"No, of course not. You look lovely," Liam said, his words short.

"You look very handsome," Fi tried, hooking her arm through his as he led her toward the field overlooking the cove, where the wedding had been set up. And he did, at that. In a dark grey suit, with a simple white shirt and a flower at his lapel, Liam looked dashing.

"Thank you." Liam's words were clipped and Fi's heart took a dive. She wanted the old easygoing Liam back.

Taking a breath, Fi looked around and smiled, pushing

her worries away. Today was about Grace and Dylan, and that was what really mattered.

Bales of hay had been set up in long rows, with tartan blankets thrown over them. An arch built of roughhewn logs, twined with twinkle lights, greens, and hundreds of flowers, stood at the end of the aisle. On the other edge of the arch, the earth dropped away to water at the cliff's edge of the cove. It was a spectacular place to marry, and Fi was glad Grace hadn't gone too fussy with the wedding. Who needed to overdesign when nature was the prettiest backdrop?

Liam slowly escorted Fi down the aisle, and she smiled at everyone, almost rolling her eyes when she saw her mum dash a tear from her eye. This felt good, she realized, being on Liam's arm in front of her friends and family.

She wished it was her wedding day.

The thought slammed into her so hard she stumbled, just a bit, and Liam held her tighter to his side, making sure she didn't fall.

"Are you all right?" Liam whispered.

"Aye," Fi said, but it was a lie. She wasn't all right. None of this was right. She was turning her back on a good man because of her own stupid fears. She could have this – this future and the life she wanted – if she'd only give Liam a chance. If she could bring herself to trust him and tell him what she really was.

They parted at the end of the aisle and Fi felt bereft at the loss of him. She didn't want to let go of his arm, or not stand by his side. But, following protocol, she walked to her side of the aisle, smiling at Dylan, who stood waiting for his love. When the crowd gasped, Fi could have cheered. Gracie had chosen just right with her dress and she looked luminous floating across the green grass – a rose blooming for her love.

Fi saw Dylan wipe a tear, as did many in the group, and she stepped forward to take Grace's flowers. Straightening, she kept a smile on her face as Flynn began the ceremony.

Wind tickled her face and Fi turned, looking down at the cove, and then back up to Liam. His eyes locked on hers as Flynn delivered his message.

"Love is a dance, the steps of which only you two will know. You may dance together, partners, and yet remain free in your own individual movements. Love ebbs and flows, much like the waves that crash on the shore below us. It's never the same each day, but rest assured, only when you truly love someone can you be free."

Liam's eyes burned into hers, and Fi's heart stopped for what felt like forever, as she lost herself in his eyes. Maybe this was what she needed to hear, she realized. That a true partner wouldn't restrict her, but would set her free. And in that moment, she decided to trust Liam with her secrets.

"Look," Keelin whispered from behind her. As Grace and Dylan were pronounced husband and wife, the cove lit from within – a brilliant blue color that only those at the cliff's edge could see. Fi blinked back tears and stole a glance at Liam, wondering what he would think of the magick displayed down below. A wide grin split his handsome face, and he seemed enraptured by what he saw. If that was truly the case, then maybe Grace was right – maybe Liam could be the man to accept all of her.

CHAPTER 38

Fi made it through the first dance before she had to step away and take a moment for herself. They'd erected a huge tent with a dance floor on the green fields by the cove, and everyone had laughed their way through the evening and now on to dancing. Fi just needed… a minute.

She needed to breathe.

There hadn't been a moment alone that she could talk to Liam all day and night, with pictures, dinner, speeches… it was just one thing after another. Now, as everyone took to the dance floor, Fi realized she needed a moment to check in with herself and her feelings. Slipping away from the dance floor, she walked the fields until she arrived at the edge of the cove. The moon, full as could be – because of *course* Grace would marry under a full moon – shone brightly off the water far below her.

"Fi."

Fi didn't turn, for a part of her had known he would

follow. Instead, she steeled herself for what would come next.

"Liam," she said, still looking down at the water. He came to stand next to her, following her gaze to the waves that crashed below.

"That's quite a drop. I hope you aren't thinking of jumping," Liam said lightly.

"No, just admiring the water. I needed a moment," Fi said with a laugh.

"Did you see the water during the ceremony?" Liam asked and Fi tore her gaze away from the water to turn and look up at him.

"Aye, I did. Did you?"

"It looked like it shone an intense blue light. But that could have been my eyes playing tricks on me."

"No, it was real."

"It's magick then. Not just a myth like the villagers say."

"Aye, it's magick," And so am I, Fi added silently. It felt good to say it, even if just in her head, she realized, and a warmth seemed to flood her.

"I kind of figured, since it tried to kill me." Liam laughed and scrubbed a hand over his face. "But this seemed a kinder side to the cove than I've experienced."

"It was. The cove glows from within in the presence of true love," Fi supplied, and Liam tilted his head at her. The moonlight lit his eyes as he studied her face.

"You believe in it then?"

"Of course." Fi took a deep breath. "And not only is the cove magick... but..."

"But what?"

"But I am as well." The world seemed to freeze for an instant, the moment hanging suspended between them as Liam's eyes held hers. She'd never in her life told another soul this secret, and her stomach turned as she waited for his response.

"You're... magick?" Liam asked, speaking slowly.

"Aye, I am. I'm part of the bloodline that runs from the magick in the cove. I'm magick, Liam." Fi blew out a breath and her palms felt clammy as she clenched her hands together.

"Like Grace, then?" Liam asked.

"No, my abilities are in a different area. Actually, one that I've fought against my whole life."

"Why? Why fight who you are?" Thank the goddess, Liam hadn't run screaming, and was listening carefully to her words.

"I didn't want to rely on my... gifts to get me by in life. So I suppressed them."

"You can suppress magick?"

"Of course. It takes work, but then it becomes routine. Except for the dreams; I can't control those."

"What do your dreams do?" Liam's eyes widened and she realized she still hadn't told him what she was.

"I'm a telepath, Liam. I can read people's minds if I want to. I also have prophetic dreams. Oh, and I can see people's auras. Kind of a mixed bag of things." Fi went still as Liam's face contorted.

"You can read minds? You could read *my* mind? But... you said you didn't know Luis was lying." Liam crossed his arms over his chest, which she now recognized to be his defensive posture.

"Please, before you get angry… will you allow me to explain? Before you judge me?" Fi pleaded, grabbing onto his arm.

"Go ahead." Liam bit out the words, and she knew he was working to keep himself under control.

"I've never wanted this ability. My mum has it as well. Since I was young, she trained me how to shield myself so I didn't hear other's thoughts. Trust me, you don't want to know the things you can pick up by accident. It's… awful. Especially as a young child. As I grew older, I became so adept at shielding myself that it became second nature. It's only when I'm really tired or my guards are down that I occasionally catch a stray thought."

"So you've never read my thoughts?"

"No, I consider it an invasion of privacy. I don't read people's minds at all. In fact…" Fi's voice caught and she turned away to look down at the water below, not wanting to see the rejection on his face. "In all my life, I've only ever told one person outside my circle about this. My first love."

"Ah," Liam said, understanding dawning on his face. "And it didn't go well?"

"He outed me to his friends and they all tore me apart at a party he was having. It was awful. I promised myself I'd never let my guard down with a man again."

"I'm starting to understand why you've kept me at arm's length."

"Nobody's even come close to threatening my carefully curated wall. Except you. You are the only person it's felt right with… and that fact terrifies me."

"You think I'll hurt you. Or you did think so. What's changed your mind?"

"Because I realized today that I do trust you. And I want a chance with you. I trust that you'll listen to me and maybe we can make a relationship work between us... and a life that we both want to live. That love doesn't have to force you to settle down or temper your dreams. Maybe, with the right partner, I really could have it all."

"Fi," Liam said, touching her for the first time, "look at me."

Fi turned and met his eyes in the moonlight.

"Yes?"

"You can read me."

"What?" Fi asked, feeling a fine trembling run through her body.

"Read me. Open yourself to me. I have nothing to hide from you," Liam promised, holding both her hands now. "Look inside me. The answer is there."

He was trusting her, Fi realized, not only with the story she'd told him about being magick, but with his innermost thoughts. Tears sprang to her eyes as she let down her shields for the first time in ages and looked inside Liam's mind.

"You love me," Fi choked out.

"Aye, I do. Even more so now that I know this extra layer of you," Liam said.

"I think I love you too. I don't know, I'm kind of a mess right now. But I know I want to give this a chance," Fi admitted, stumbling over her words. "But it slammed into me when we were walking down the aisle together that I wanted a chance with you. A real one."

"We can have that. But it starts with trusting each other. Will you trust me, Fi? To love you and be your partner? So that we can be together and explore the world? To design a future that looks exactly like we want it to?"

"I do," Fi whispered, and then his lips were on hers and nothing else mattered. She'd finally found a safe harbor with the one man who would weather all the storms with her. Pulling back, she smiled up at him.

"Look!" Liam said, pulling her into his arm so they could turn and look at the glow emanating from the water below them. "It's meant to be. The cove says so."

"Aye, that it does."

"It was worth it trying to kill me, then, as it led me to you," Liam decided and Fi threw back her head and laughed.

And as simply as that, Fi finally embraced her magick.

EPILOGUE

"*T*hat's a fine streak of luck you've had, Mr. Murphy," Cait said, studying the leather-bound book she'd plopped onto the bar.

The entire pub laughed as Mr. Murphy crowed in delight.

"I can't believe you'd bet on me. Me own mum." Fi shook her head sadly, as if to ask what the world was coming to.

"Then you don't know your mum very well," Cait shot back, and Fi laughed.

"How'd you come to pick that date, Mr. Murphy?" Liam asked.

"Weddings make people feel romantic. It seemed like a suitable day," Mr. Murphy said, tugging at his newsboy cap as his cheeks blushed pink.

"Well, you've won yourself a fine pot of money, you have. I think the whole town bet on it," Cait said, sliding him another Guinness. "What will you do with your winnings this time?"

"Well, I've been thinking about that..." Mr. Murphy ducked his head. "And I've a favor to ask of you."

"Go ahead," Cait nodded.

"I'm wondering if you'll take me to see the elephants. A safari like you all were talking about a while back. I'm too old to go by myself, but I'd dearly love to see them before I leave this world."

Cait's mouth dropped open, then she turned a steely gaze toward the kitchen, where Shane stood with a towel draped across his shoulder. His mouth quirked with a small smile, but he said nothing.

"Oh, you're a wily one, Shane, aren't you?" Cait called, and Shane laughed, shrugging his shoulders. He knew, just as everyone else in the bar did, that Mr. Murphy was the man Cait couldn't say no to. It seemed she would be taking a vacation no matter what.

"Is that a yes?" Mr. Murphy asked hopefully.

"Aye – but *only* if I can find someone to cover the pub," Cait said, seeing a way out.

"I'll do that for you, Mum," Fi said cheerfully, smiling in her seat next to Liam, his arm casually around her waist. "I'm sure Liam could help, as well."

"I've tended a pub or two in my time," Liam agreed.

"It'll be fun. And it will give me some time to haul all those boxes from your house to mine." Fi layered it on, knowing how much her mother wanted the clutter out of her house.

"Oh, you're a sneaky one too," Cait said.

"So? Do we get to see the elephants then?" Mr. Murphy asked, his voice tremulous as he leaned forward.

"We do, Mr. Murphy, we do," Cait said, and the entire

pub cheered once more. Mr. Murphy was so delighted he almost toppled off his stool. Shane, ducking through the passthrough, picked Cait up and spun her around.

"I like your parents together," Liam said into Fi's ear. "They're a good fit for each other."

"They are. They balance each other."

"Think we can balance each other?"

"I think we can do a lot of things together," Fi said, then blushed when Liam whispered a decidedly naughty suggestion in her ear.

"What is with you and that latex dress?" Fi laughed.

"Humor me," Liam whispered, and Fi felt her insides flash liquid heat.

"I'm glad I didn't throw it out," Fi said, and laughed when Liam clutched his heart.

"Please don't."

"No, I see that I need to keep it around."

"You really do. You can wear it while we paint your flat. I bet it cleans easily," Liam said.

Fi laughed. They were staying in Grace's Cove until her parents came back from the trip, something Shane had run past her earlier this week, knowing he could convince Cait to travel. Liam would continue overseeing the community center project and Fi would run the pub and work on her new house. They hadn't openly discussed living together, but Liam's stuff had already taken up residence in her flat and instead of feeling constricting, it felt... right.

Fi, after a few difficult nights, had come to Liam with a plan. At first, he'd worried for her.

"You know I want you to be happy. And I think this is great for you, but I want you to be sure."

"It's still my career; I'm just shifting it a bit. Which means I can work from home or wherever we travel to," Fi said.

"I can see you sitting in the galley of the boat, typing away furiously while the boat rocks. Or tucked away in some stone castle in the hills of Slovenia, translating while a storm rages outside," Liam said with a smile.

"I want to do this. I want to try. For me. Because I think it will be fun. And, frankly, so long as I get to travel with you, I'll be happy. It's the travel that's important to me. But if we're both traveling constantly, apart from each other, I don't think that will be good for us."

"Translating novels it is, then?" Liam had studied her face.

"Aye. I've a friend who has already lined me up with my first two novels. Romances, at that." Fi had laughed at Liam's expression.

"Hmm, do the heroines wear latex dresses?"

"They might. I haven't read them yet."

"Then I'm in. This is going to be a perfect future for us."

SECRET CHAPTER

"I have a surprise for you! As a gift to you, here is a secret chapter that is a prequel to a book of my heart, Ms. Bitch. This chapter is not included in the actual book, so I hope you enjoy!" Tricia.

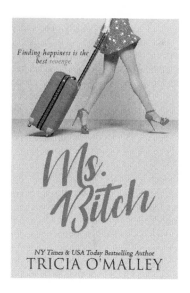

Today was *the* day. The day she'd never spent too much time dreaming about, but had always assumed she'd partake in at least once in her life.

Tess rolled over in the hotel bed, the sheet soft and cool against her skin, and propped herself on her elbow to study her fiancé's face. At thirty, Gabe Campbell was handsome in a guy-next-door kind of way, with soulful eyes, a quirky smile, and was the life of every party. Tess had been drawn into his gravitational force since the moment she'd met him, and he'd decided she was going to be his next girlfriend. It had happened so quickly – from single to living together – that Tess had barely had time to think. She loved it, though. It was nice to be the center of someone's universe.

For once she hadn't felt so alone.

"Hey babe," Gabe said, blinking awake with a smile at her touch. "We're getting married today."

"That we are," Tess said, smiling down at him, though her stomach twisted. Just nerves, she told herself. Getting married in New Orleans had been something they'd looked forward to for months now and was a destination wedding dream-come-true for the both of them.

When they'd come to New Orleans together three years ago, it had been their first trip together as a couple. Tess had a deep love for travel, and was slowly introducing Gabe to her passion for exploring new places. Never one for expanding much outside his comfort zone, Gabe had stuck to trips to his family cabin in the northern woods of Wisconsin, or an occasional road trip to see one of his favorite bands play. He'd never even been on a plane, something which had surprised Tess when he'd first told her. She'd held his hand as the plane touched down on the runway, soothing the nervous tapping of his knee against hers.

Gabe's eyes had lit up when he'd first stepped into the French Quarter where music and mayhem called to him. He'd loved the messiness of it all, as the French Quarter didn't try to be pretentious. Instead, like a sultry burlesque dancer, the city put her wares on display and insisted that people take her as she was. And take her, they did. Gabe and Tess had stormed the French Quarter, eating and drinking their way through the town, and reveling in all the secrets the city had to share. From ghost tours, steamboat rides, to tiny jazz bands tucked into tiny jazz bars, they tried it all. It had been a perfect weekend – silly and fun and decadent – and they'd come home even more excited to plan their next trip.

From that weekend forward, Tess had begun to look to a future with Gabe. Sure, they had their moments – what couple didn't – but she thought they'd be able to figure out their problems and take on the world together. And really, just because Gabe had never met a bar he didn't like, didn't mean his drinking was all that bad. They lived in a state known for corner bars and long cold winters where there wasn't much else to do but have a few cocktails.

When he'd gotten down on one knee and proposed, Tess had said yes, *of course* she would marry him. And now the day had finally come, one which they'd planned with giddy expectation for months now.

That's all it was – just nerves – Tess thought. She studied her soon-to-be husband. Neither of them particularly enjoyed being the center of attention, and yet they'd ended up having one hundred people RSVP to their destination wedding. This whole week she'd been managing last-minute details all while traveling and trying to stay organized.

"I'm just going to shower and then off to meet my brothers," Gabe said, striding naked from the bed to the bathroom. "I have to be out of here by when?"

"Um, what time is it now?"

"It's seven-thirty."

"Hair and make-up is coming at eight."

"Why so early?"

"They are doing all the girls and some family. They just need time."

"Guess I'll just hit up a bar with my brothers then."

Tess opened her mouth to say something and then shut it, closing her eyes for a moment and taking a deep breath. Rolling from the bed she began to put the room to order, making sure that the lavish suite would be suitable for her friends that would be joining her to get ready.

"Today is going to be so much fun," Tess said, when Gabe came out wrapped in a towel, "I can't wait for the second line."

"I know! Our own parade! It's going to be badass." Gabe did a little shimmy across the hotel room to the closet and pulled out his clothes. "None of our friends back home have had a wedding like this. Ours is going to be one everyone talks about for ages." Gabe loved nothing more than being better than other people.

"Well, it's New Orleans. It's going to be a fun weekend no matter what. But to give everyone a chance to be in a parade? Yeah, that's pretty damn cool."

"It would have been better if we hadn't had to put up with all the hassle that came with planning it. Especially from Vicki," Gabe said, referring to her sister. Tess wondered what hassle he'd dealt with, as he literally only had to pick up his tux and show up at the wedding day. Vicki had told Gabe that wedding planning was a woman's job, and he'd taken that and run with it. Frankly all Gabe cared about was having a big party and making sure *their* wedding was the best. Vicki had been the one to complain about all the details.

Not to mention she didn't want Tess to marry Gabe.

"I think that's probably just normal with planning weddings. Everyone wants a say." Tess shrugged.

"Well, she certainly had hers. Hopefully she'll back off now," Gabe shrugged as he zipped up his suit bag and walked across the room. Sliding his lips over hers, he held her close for a moment. "Next time I see you, you'll be Mrs. Campbell."

"Eeek! Crazy." Tess laughed and waved goodbye to him, her stomach flipping in knots. Whether it was nervousness over being the center of attention or because she was actually getting married, she wasn't feeling that well. Finding Advil, Tess took it with a cup of coffee while she stared out the window at the street below. By the time the knock sounded on the door – Tess was ready to face the day.

Voices crashed through the room and in moments it was a blur of faces, chatter, and platters of food arriving. Soon enough, the makeup girls had set up stations and Tess waited patiently for her turn. She was going last, so as not to mess her makeup up, and now she sat quietly in the corner of the couch.

"I'm leaving after this," Vicki said, ducking her head and glaring at the hair stylist who was wielding a bobby pin in the air.

"Why?" Tess wondered. Vicki, her only family in the room, was meant to spend the day helping her get ready.

"Your aunt is throwing a brunch for everyone, so I'm going to go," Vicki said, standing and patting the simple chic French twist the stylist had tucked her blonde hair into. "I'll see you at the hotel for pictures."

"Oh, well, okay. Tell everyone I said hello," Tess said to Vicki's back as she retreated through the door. Mae, her maid-of-honor met her eyes across the room and shook her head in annoyance.

Tess rolled her eyes and then smiled at Mae who came to crouch by her side.

"Hey, are you okay? You're pretty quiet today."

"Yeah, I'm fine I guess. I just have an upset stomach. Must be nerves."

"Are you nervous about getting married or just the day?"

"I think just the day. Being the center of attention. I don't know. I'm sure that's all it is. A lot of planning all coming to a head."

"If you want to call it off, you can, you know." Mae's eyes were serious in her pretty face.

"Mae! No, I don't. God, could you imagine? He already had a meltdown when I pretended to call it off at the airport."

As a joke, Tess had pulled Gabe aside before they

checked in for their flight and told him she couldn't marry him. She'd done it only to distract him from his cousin – who had previously been unable to attend their wedding – sneaking up behind him in the airport as a surprise. She hadn't expected the sheer terror on Gabe's face, nor the fact that he would sweat completely through his jacket. Obviously, the man loved her.

And wasn't that just what she needed? Tess had been looking for someone to love her – to start a family with – for years. Ever since she'd lost her parents, it felt like she had an aching void in her life that she hadn't known how to fill. Until Gabe came along with his constant attention and charming words. It had been kind of like being run over with a steamroller, and since that time he'd consumed her life.

"Tess, are you ready?" The makeup artist called to her and Tess turned to Mae.

"Yes, I'm ready."

The day flashed by in a blur of moments. She met Gabe for their first look on the rooftop balcony of the hotel overlooking New Orleans. The photographer had followed them up there to capture the moment, but all Tess had eyes for was Gabe.

He climbed the stairs to the balcony and when his eyes found her, waiting in her wedding dress, her hair done *just so* – her heart fell when a grimace crossed his face. He must have seen it in her look, because he quickly grinned widely at her and strode across the roof-deck to hug her close.

"You don't like the dress," Tess whispered in his ear.

"It wasn't something I expected you to choose," Gabe

admitted, before pulling back and smiling widely at the photographer. Tess glanced down at her dress. Maybe he was right. At the time, she'd thought the white satin V-neck gown with sequins at the waist and antique sequin detailing down the back would fit the vibe of New Orleans. Now, she realized she'd missed the mark and should have chosen something more her. Biting back her disappointment, she smiled for the camera as Gabe pressed a kiss to her cheek.

"Don't worry, babe, you look lovely. Really," Gabe promised, "You didn't say anything about how I look."

Conscious of the photographer, Tess stepped back and looked Gabe up and down before letting out a long wolf whistle. His delighted grin said it all and he pushed his shoulders back for the photographer. Ever aware of his looks, Gabe posed with confidence as Tess mustered up the courage to walk out in front of a crowd in a dress her soon-to-be husband clearly didn't like.

The first look pictures complete, they met up with their bridal party who sent up cheers when they arrived in the gleaming lobby. Champagne was popped, and Tess gratefully accept her glass of liquid courage, the bubbles pinging their way down her throat to her knotted stomach. The group cheerfully wound their way through the quarter, taking pictures as they went, until they landed at the hotel where Tess and Gabe would marry in an outdoor courtyard.

Time stood still, as Gabe left her. Music swelled, and everyone began their walk. Mae turned and shot Tess a questioning look. Tess shook her head no, and then yes, and then pasted the brightest smile she could muster on her face. Deciding to believe her, Mae looked forward and made her way down the aisle on the arm of Gabe's brother. Thirty minutes later, she'd vowed before everyone to trust, honor, and love the man who stood before her. The moment slowed, as she looked into his eyes, and every ounce of Tess willed this marriage to work.

At the very least, to prove Vicki wrong.

Despite her misgivings, Tess laughed as one of New Orleans's best brass bands struck a raucous celebratory tune as they spilled out onto Bourbon Street. Following the band, the wedding party led their guests in a parade that stopped time. Second line parades were a notorious New Orleans's tradition, and the music from the band had people running out from the restaurants and stores to cheer. Finally, Tess felt the tension that that had plagued her all day ease. She laughed, twisting her parasol high in the air, and danced down the street holding Gabe's hand.

"As I give you my hand to hold, so I give you my life to keep."

The vow flashed through her mind as Gabe grabbed her and twirled so that her dress fanned out around her. Surprising her, he dipped Tess in the street and kissed her to the onlookers' cheers.

This was the man she loved. Certain that this was the start of their new life, Tess kissed him back, hopeful that the best was yet to come.

Available as an e-book, Hardback, Paperback, Audio or Large Print.
Read Today

MS. BITCH

FINDING HAPPINESS IS THE BEST REVENGE

From the outside, it seems thirty-six-year-old Tess Campbell has it all. A happy marriage, a successful career as a novelist, and an exciting cross-country move ahead. Tess has always played by the rules and it seems like life is good.

Except it's not. Life is a bitch. And suddenly so is Tess.

"Ms. Bitch is sunshine in a book! An uplifting story of fighting your way through heartbreak and making your own version of happily-ever-after."
~Ann Charles, USA Today Bestselling Author of the Deadwood Mystery Series

"Authentic and relatable, Ms. Bitch packs an emotional punch. By the end, I was crying happy tears and ready to pack my bags in search of my best life."
-Annabel Chase, author of the Starry Hollow Witches series

"It's easy to be brave when you have a lot of support in your life, but it takes a special kind of courage to forge a new path when you're alone. Tess is the heroine I hope I'll be if my life ever crumbles down around me. Ms. Bitch is a journey of determination, a study in self-love, and a hope for second chances. I could not put it down!"

-Renee George, USA Today Bestselling Author of the Nora Black Midlife Psychic Mysteries

"I don't know where to start listing all the reasons why you should read this book. It's empowering. It's fierce. It's about loving yourself enough to build the life you want. It was honest, and raw, and real and I just...loved it so much!"

– Sara Wylde, author of Fat

Available as an e-book, Hardback, Paperback, Audio or Large Print.
Read Today

AFTERWORD

Ireland holds a special place in my heart – a land of dreamers and for dreamers. There's nothing quite like cozying up next to a fire in a pub and listening to a session or having a cup of tea while the rain mists outside the window. I'll forever be enchanted by her rocky shores and I hope you enjoy this series as much as I enjoyed writing it. Thank you for taking part in my world, I hope that my stories bring you great joy.

Have you read books from my other series? Join our little community by signing up for my newsletter for updates on island-living, fun giveaways, and how to follow me on social media!
http://eepurl.com/1LAiz.

or at my website
www.triciaomalley.com

Please consider leaving a review! Your review helps others to take a chance on my stories. I really appreciate your help!

THE ISLE OF DESTINY SERIES

ALSO BY TRICIA O'MALLEY

Stone Song

Sword Song

Spear Song

Sphere Song

———————

"Love this series. I will read this multiple times. Keeps you on the edge of your seat. It has action, excitement and romance all in one series."- Amazon Review

Available in audio, e-book & paperback!

Read Now

THE ALTHEA ROSE SERIES

ALSO BY TRICIA O'MALLEY

One Tequila

Tequila for Two

Tequila Will Kill Ya (Novella)

Three Tequilas

Tequila Shots & Valentine Knots (Novella)

Tequila Four

A Fifth of Tequila

A Sixer of Tequila

Seven Deadly Tequilas

"Not my usual genre but couldn't resist the Florida Keys setting. I was hooked from the first page. A fun read with just the right amount of crazy! Will definitely follow this series."- Amazon Review

Available in audio, e-book & paperback!

Read Now

AUTHOR'S NOTE

Thank you for taking a chance on my books; it means the world to me. Writing novels came by way of a tragedy that turned into something beautiful and larger than itself (see: *The Stolen Dog*). Since that time, I've changed my career, put it all on the line, and followed my heart.

Thank you for taking part in the worlds I have created; I hope you enjoy it.

I would be honored if you left a review online. It helps other readers to take a chance on my work.

As always, you can reach me at
info@triciaomalley.com
or feel free to visit my website at
www.triciaomalley.com.

AUTHOR'S ACKNOWLEDGEMENT

First, and foremost, I'd like to thank my family and friends for their constant support, advice, and ideas. You've all proven to make a difference on my path. And, to my beta readers, I love you for all of your support and fascinating feedback!

And last, but never least, my two constant companions as I struggle through words on my computer each day - Briggs and Blue.

Made in the USA
Las Vegas, NV
17 July 2022

51758748R00169